Abby—Secret at Cutter Grove

SOUTH SEAS ADVENTURES

Abby
Secret at Cutter Grove

PAMELA WALLS

TYNDALE
KIDS

TYNDALE HOUSE PUBLISHERS, INC.
WHEATON, ILLINOIS

Visit Tyndale's exciting Web site at www.tyndale.com

ISBN 0-8423-3629-X

Printed in the United States of America

08 07 06 05 04 03 02 01
10 9 8 7 6 5 4 3 2 1

DEDICATED TO GREGG (MY SWEET BROTHER),
LYNETTE, JESSIE, AND NICOLE;
AND ELIZABETH, DAUGHTER OF MY HEART.

*"You will know them by their fruits. Grapes are
not gathered from thorn bushes, nor figs from thistles,
are they? Even so, every good tree bears good fruit;
but the bad tree bears bad fruit."*
Matthew 7:16-17, NASB

Chapter One

June 1848

Abby Kendall shaded her eyes from the glare of Oahu's white sand beach. "Home!" She almost sang the word as she leaned over the ship's railing.

When Duncan MacIndou, the Scottish captain of the *Fair Winds,* gave the order to drop anchor, everyone on board scurried to do his bidding. But Abby was too entranced with her first view of the island to notice. The Hawaiian trade winds whipped stray ringlets from the 13-year-old's long cinnamon braid as she drank in Kailua Bay's arc of bleached sand fringed with swaying palm trees.

"At long last," she murmured, thinking how wonderful it would be to see Ma, Pa, and Uncle Samuel again. Would they notice how different she was now—how much more grown up she'd become since her adventure in California?

Duncan cleared his throat as he strolled up beside her, white teeth gleaming through the dark handlebar moustache. His cotton shirtsleeves were rolled past his elbows, revealing muscled arms, well tanned from the three-week sail. "Well, lassie," he said, "ye've finally rrreturned."

Abby gazed up at his one steel gray eye and the black patch that covered the other. The kindhearted Scotsman had been their friend and chaperon through journeys to parts of Hawaii and California, and she loved him dearly. For months she'd shared what was on her heart with Duncan, and it was natural to do so now. The words bubbled up. "Soon we'll see Ma and Pa."

After several months of worrying whether their ma would recover from a mysterious illness, Abby and her eight-year-old sister, Sarah, had finally received word that they could come home. Three months earlier Ma and Pa had insisted the girls leave the island of Oahu with Abby's best friend, Luke Quiggley; Duncan; and their new 10-year-old Hawaiian friend and traveling companion, Kini, so they wouldn't catch her fever.

But there had been more in store for them in California than anyone could have expected. While they were there, the gold rush had begun. Abby had started her own Rich Diggin's Bakery in the wilderness, and she and Luke had uncovered a kidnapping ring. She'd also found a doctor who'd agreed to come back to their side of the island, where no doctor yet lived. Now if anyone ever got as sick as Ma had been, there'd be a physician to help.

Duncan raked a hand through his dark hair. "I'll be looking for new crew rrright away." His face was serious as he scanned the beach, then added quietly, "But 'twill be hard to rrreplace ye."

"Duncan, I hadn't thought about that." Abby had been so intent on seeing her parents, she hadn't stopped to realize that this homecoming meant saying good-bye to her dear friend.

"Aye, 'tis been on me mind often this past week. I'll drop ye and the others off and head out to Kauai as soon as possible."

"I . . . I guess that means we won't be able to help you find your father's trail." Suddenly Abby wondered about her future. She'd return to her uncle's quiet ranch, set high in the hills and off the beaten track, while Duncan would sail away to solve the mystery of his father's disappearance—which had occurred over 30 years ago.

In the past few months, Abby had learned to love sailing, traveling, adventure. And Luke seemed to thrive on it, too. But with Duncan leaving them behind, their hope for future adventures looked bleak.

Abby gripped the railing until her knuckles turned white. "Duncan, if you go off without us, we'll never know how your search ended."

Duncan placed a warm hand on her shoulder and squeezed briefly. "For a private detective who's always worked alone, lassie, I've grrrown awfully fond of ye and the others. I admit, I'll be lonely without ye."

Abby bit her lip. She knew Duncan had come to

think of them as family, especially Luke, who looked up to him.

A sigh escaped his lips. "'Twill be an adjustment after all these months together, but I don't know if I'll be coming back. Who knows where the path will lead? But I do know I have to discover what happened to me da."

Abby nodded sadly. "I'll be praying you find out, Duncan." After all, it was because of Abby that he'd found his father's diary, filled with clues about Ian MacIndou's last days.

When the Scotsman bent down and gave her a hug, Abby clung to him. Her heart felt sad, as if something had gone unexpectedly wrong.

Seconds later Duncan was called away, and Abby turned back to view the shore. Her cornflower blue eyes took interest when a group of people emerged from the tree line and headed toward the water.

A large Hawaiian woman dressed in a red ankle-length muumuu led the pack. Her wavy long hair was snow-white, and Abby grinned with recognition. It *had* to be Olani, her dear friend and the chieftess who lived in Kailua.

"Olani!" Abby yelled enthusiastically over the sound of the crashing surf. She waved her arm until the group on shore noticed her and began waving back. "It's Olani," she cried, and Sarah and Kini broke into grins as they joined her at the railing.

Behind her, Abby heard the sound of the anchor splashing into the bay waters. She'd had every intention of looking her best when she arrived, but they'd worked all morning and the sun had been hot. She now stood barefoot, dressed simply in a yellow cotton blouse and blue chambray skirt.

"I see Mama!" Sarah squealed as she jumped up and down. Sarah's cornsilk blonde hair had lightened even more during the weeks of sailing. Her thin frame looked tanned and healthy.

"It can't be Ma," Abby said. "She couldn't know we'd be arriving today. She's at Uncle Samuel's ranch in the hills." But her gaze roamed hungrily over the group anyway.

One man stood taller than everyone else on shore. Abby's heart thumped against her ribs. The wavy, dark blond hair and familiar walk—it *was* Pa! And walking beside him was Ma!

"Good eyes, Sarah!" Abby said as a bubble of joy bloomed in her chest. The weeks of longing to see Ma alive and well spurred Abby on without thinking. She dived overboard into the turquoise water. For a split second, she basked in the warm, welcoming waters of home that pulsed and surged around her. Then she struck out for shore with sure strokes in spite of her long skirt.

Sarah watched, then stamped her foot on the teak deck. "Abby Kendall, you come back here," she demanded. "That's not fair!"

Abby turned back and saw Duncan laughing as he put an arm around Sarah's shoulders. "Lassie, yer sister is guided by her hearrrt."

"Look out below!" 14-year-old Luke yelled as he waved from the top of the rigging. He'd apparently seen Charlotte and Thomas Kendall, too. Abby's eyes widened as Luke suddenly let go and plunged 20 feet down, narrowly missing the deck and slicing into the briny deep like a jackknife into cream. When he surfaced, he sputtered, his hair glinting with sun-blond streaks as it lay plastered to his forehead. When Luke grinned impishly at her, she knew the race was on!

Abby quickly turned back toward shore and kicked hard. On land, Luke always outraced her—unless he let her win. She'd inherited Ma's weak legs and ran slowly. But in the water, she had a fighting chance. She skimmed over the blue surface, her arms pulling and legs churning like a windmill.

The Kailua beach grew closer and closer. Briefly opening her eyes underwater, Abby could see the sand swirling just 10 feet below. As the ocean grazed the bottom, it curled into a wave, and she rode the swell toward shore. It swept up onto the beach, depositing her on the squishy sand, where two strong hands instantly gripped her under the arms and helped her to her feet.

"Pa!" Abby flung herself against his dry chest.

Thomas Kendall stood barefoot in the lacy surf, gazing down tenderly at his tanned, water-drenched daughter. "You're a sight for sore eyes, Princess!" he said, picking her up in a huge hug.

As Pa's warm arms circled her, she kissed him on his bristly cheek, asking, "Where's Ma?"

Charlotte Kendall stood at the edge of the surf, holding her skirts ankle high so they wouldn't get wet. But the minute Abby rocketed into her arms, Charlotte dropped her skirts and embraced her daughter tightly. Neither could speak. The tide swept up their legs twice while Abby sniffed back tears, inhaling Ma's familiar lilac scent. After a long moment, she stepped back to gaze into Ma's pretty face, framed by mink-brown hair. "Are you well, Ma?"

"As good as gold," Ma said laughing, as she planted a kiss on Abby's salty cheek.

Abby's eyes gleamed. "How did you know?"

"Know what?" Ma asked, her brown eyes questioning.

"That I brought gold."

Pa chuckled. "Did you find a pirate's treasure, Abby?"

Luke emerged dripping and joined the conversation. "Better than that. She started her own business in the middle of the California gold rush!"

While Luke squeezed the ocean out of his shirt, Pa responded. "The gold rush? We've just heard about it. Sounds incredible, unbelievable! But how could you be part of the gold rush when you were staying with Luke's aunt in Pueblo de San Jose?" Pa's eyebrows narrowed over blue eyes, which bored into her.

Swallowing, Abby explained. "Mrs. Gronen was unkind, Pa. She almost slapped Sarah in the face just because Sarah dropped her silver."

Ma's face tightened with concern. "Is Sarah all right?"

"Abby took good care of her," Luke said proudly. "And she brought you a surprise—something important for the ranch."

Charlotte and Thomas eyed each other soberly. Thomas was just about to open his mouth when a young voice cried out over the pounding surf. "Mama!"

Sarah was holding Sandy, Luke's new yellow puppy, in her arms and riding over the swells in the ship's rowboat, which was just cresting over the wave. Kai and Liho, the two *kanaka* sailors they'd picked up in California, were rowing hard. Pa hurried to catch the little boat as it washed ashore and then pushed it up the beach with the help of Duncan, who'd jumped out. Dr. Sheldon Armstrong, who'd come from California to set up practice in Hawaii, and Kini watched from their seats in the skiff as Pa lifted a dry Sarah from it.

After a fierce hug, Pa thrust Sarah into Ma's waiting arms. Clinging tightly, Sarah piped up loudly, "And I made it back in time for my birthday, Mama!"

"What a happy day!" Olani exclaimed as she and her friends gathered around the returning crew. One at a time, she gathered each child into her

PAMELA WALLS

ample arms for a hug while Ma and Pa stood, waiting to greet Luke and Kini. But with Abby, Olani bent down and rubbed noses in the intimate Hawaiian greeting.

"My *nani*-hair returns!" she said, glowing. "And you bring joy with you." Olani picked up Abby's straggly, unkempt braid and winced. "But your *nani*-hair looks broken," she said with a grin. "We go fix?"

Surrounded by friends and family, Abby felt her heart swell just like the ocean wave had. Ma appeared fit as a fiddle, perhaps a bit thinner, but alive and rosy. God had answered all her prayers.

"Pa," Abby said, remembering her manners, "we've brought back Dr. Armstrong from San Francisco. He's going to set up an office on this side of the island." Abby almost crowed with satisfaction. "Now whenever anyone in Kailua is sick, there'll be a doctor here to help!"

Pa looked genuinely shocked, and Ma beamed at her. "Is this your doing?" she asked.

Abby nodded as handshakes and introductions were made. "But we brought back something else," she said, eyes bright with anticipation. Pa would jump and shout when she told him that she'd earned enough money for Uncle Samuel to buy his ranch! Now Rassmassen, their threatening neighbor, couldn't force them off the land as he hoped to. With the recent Great Mahele, or land act, Uncle Samuel was going to have to pay for the land he'd originally been given. Abby had worked her fingers to the bone to earn enough gold to save the ranch. This was her moment to tell Ma that she would now have a permanent place to call home.

"Pa, we've also brought you enough gold to buy the ranch." The words tumbled out in a rush. "You see, I started a bakery in California. And the miners loved my pies and breads. They paid me in gold, and I made hundreds!"

Pa's eyes went wide. "Hundreds of pies?"

"And hundreds of dollars!" Abby answered. She waited for the response she'd been dreaming about.

But Pa didn't grin and shout like she'd imagined. A cloud seemed to cast his face in shadows as his forehead puckered. Finally, a weary sigh escaped. "Abby girl, the reason we're here at Kailua beach is because the ranch . . . it's gone. We've been living with Olani since . . ."

"Since Rassmassen bought it," Ma finished, "and kicked us out of Uncle Samuel's home."

Chapter Two

Abby's stomach twisted at the terrible news. Her gaze wove between her parents. "I'm too late?"

Ma's arm encircled her shoulders and tucked Abby against her side. "No, sweetheart, you're right on time. God brought you safely home, and He must have a reason to move us on from this lovely place. Maybe it's to find a better place . . . to call home." Abby heard the catch in her mother's voice and looked up sharply. But Charlotte Kendall was smiling again.

Duncan cleared his throat. "So ye've no place to settle?"

"No." Pa scrubbed his cheek with one hand.

Uncle Samuel, Pa's older brother who'd been silent up to this point, now spoke up. "But if Abby's brought money, then there's nothing to stop us from searching for another ranch to buy."

"Ma deserves it," Abby said quietly, thinking of how Ma had left her home to come west with Pa. How she'd worked hard to make their little rented cottage in California into a home, but that hadn't lasted either. And just when they thought they'd live at Uncle Samuel's ranch forever, it had been snatched away.

Olani spoke up in her lilting voice. "My cousin, Malama—she lives on Kauai where they grow sugarcane. She is distant cousin, but she visits me sometimes. She tells us there is much river, much rain, much sunshine for farming. Maybe you can go see her?"

Duncan twirled his handlebar moustache absently. "Kauai—that's the very place I'm going next. I want to pick up the trail of me da's last days in Hawaii." He cocked his head at Pa and continued. "I can certainly offer your family a free ride there. . . . In fact, I need extra hands to sail."

Abby held her breath, hoping against hope that Pa would say yes.

Uncle Samuel, a biologist who was a slightly older version of Pa, responded first. "It's called the 'Garden Isle' for a reason, Thomas. I've never been there, but I know it's home to the growing sugar industry in the Pacific. Maybe we could investigate plantation life, see if we want to start our own sugar trade?"

"Well," Pa said slowly, turning the idea over in his mind, "we have been praying for a direction. . . . Why don't we visit Olani's cousin and see what we can learn?"

When Duncan and Pa shook hands, relief

flooded Abby. *Lord,* she prayed, *our good-byes are put off again. And maybe Luke and I can help Duncan pick up his father's trail on Kauai!*

Luke did a handstand, and Sandy, his pup, ran circles around him. When the short-legged canine tripped, then plowed nose first into the sand and sneezed, everyone laughed.

"Come," Olani beckoned. "You eat one fine *luau* with us before you leave. I will miss you, so we send you off with roasted pig and breadfruit in your belly!" Luke's eyes lit up as he whooped again, and Abby laughed. He was the hungriest boy she'd ever known.

Everyone followed Olani over the low sand dune toward her fishing village. From the back of the group, Abby could hear the gracious chieftess speaking. "Dr. Armstrong," Olani said, "we need a physician here, so we gladly help you build your office."

The young doctor grinned at the kind chieftess. "I think," he said, looking up at the swaying coconut trees, grass huts, and smiling Hawaiian villagers, "I have just arrived in paradise."

Abby lifted her wet skirt away from her legs as she followed the others over the sand. She'd fallen behind as usual, but Luke stopped and waited for her to catch up.

"Looks like we're headed on a new adventure," he said, pushing his drying hair out of his green eyes. "But this time on a full belly—and with the whole family." Then as a new thought hit him, Luke scowled. "You don't think your ma is gonna make us do schoolwork, do you?"

Abby laughed as she glanced up at her best friend. They'd met in Pueblo de San Jose, California, when he'd come west three years earlier to live with his aunt, Dagmar Gronen, after his parents' deaths. Though still a kid at heart, Luke had grown as tall and as wiry as some men. He loved to move. Abby knew he'd rather be fishing or plowing than studying math. Though he never quit teasing her about the pictures she drew or the poetry she wrote, she knew he admired her for her "book learning."

"Shhh!" Abby cautioned. "Maybe Ma'll forget about school."

"I hope not!" Kini came up behind them. "I be learning how to read good."

Abby turned and smiled at the Hawaiian boy. "What are you doing walking back here all by yourself?" she asked.

Kini scuffed the sand with his bare toes and looked down. "This be your family, Abby . . . not mine."

Abby and Luke frowned at each other. "No, Kini. My family is your family, too," Abby said gently.

"Let's get to the feast, Kini," Luke offered. "Maybe Olani will have my favorite *purple* thing to eat—*poi!*"

Kini and Abby giggled, knowing how much Luke hated the sour taro root.

As the two boys hurried forward, Abby wondered
if Kini would ever feel at home with her family.
Months earlier he'd rescued Luke and Abby from
the sacred pits, and possible death, on the island of
Lanai. Kini's grandfather, who ruled the popula-
tion, still worshipped the old Hawaiian gods and
lived by the ancient rules of *kapu*. When Kini had
risked setting Luke and Abby free, he'd broken his
grandfather's rules. Although Abby knew Kini's
mother loved him, now, because of his daring deed,
he was an outcast! "Poor Kini," she whispered to
herself. "Can he ever go home again?"

How lonely he must feel! Right then Abby vowed
to do all she could to make him happy. She was so
immersed in thought as she watched the ground for
sharp kiawe thorns that she never noticed her father
walking back toward her. She almost bumped into
him. "Pa!"

Thomas Kendall grinned down at her, his hair
shiny in the sunlight. "Oh, Abby, your mother and I
have missed you girls. I'm amazed to think you
started your own business. I want to hear all about
it over dinner tonight." He let out a slow chuckle
and gave her braid a playful yank. "I have to admit,
your behavior reminds me of someone else."

"Who, Pa?" Abby looked up into his face. His
smiles had made her hope she wouldn't get in trouble for leaving Mrs. Gronen's.

"You remind me of me. I've always loved a good
challenge. I believe you share my quest for adven-

ture." Then his vivid blue eyes grew serious. "I know your mother and I weren't with you in Pueblo de San Jose, so you couldn't ask us for help. And I know you did the best you could. But I don't want any more traipsing off without my permission, understand?"

"Yes, Pa." As they hiked together, Pa wrapped an arm around her shoulders and pulled her close. Abby breathed in his familiar scent that reminded her of warm raisins. It had been so long since she'd seen his clean-shaven face. "You did a good job of taking care of Sarah, Princess," he said. "Your ma and I are grateful."

"Oh, you're welcome, Pa."

As they headed toward the festivities, Abby didn't mention what a relief it was to hand that job back to Ma.

The dawning sun rose over Kailua Bay the next morning when Abby and the others took leave of Olani and rowed out to the *Fair Winds*.

Olani waved tearfully from the beach. She had made them promise to come back and visit. Now her lilting voice, which carried over the waves, was full of love. "*Alooo-ha!*"

As Abby and Luke untied the sails and began heaving them aloft, she turned back to shore for one last look. Olani stood with her motherly arm around Dr. Armstrong. "Look," Abby said to Luke as they pulled at the lines together. "I think Dr. Armstrong has found a home."

Luke nodded, sweat already glistening on his upper lip with the effort. Kai and Liho had promised to help sail the ship to Kauai with Duncan, but then they planned to return to their families. Kai was aloft tarring the shrouds, the ropes attached to the ship's side that ran to the masthead to steady the mast. Liho was busy below, storing the food Olani had sent with them.

Ma cuddled Sarah in her lap as they sat on the bulkhead and watched the activities. Pa and Uncle Samuel tried to help but managed to get in the way. But Abby and Luke knew exactly what to do after sailing across the wide Pacific.

Soon the sails caught the gentle morning breeze, and Duncan steered the ship into the rising sun. Abby retrieved her journal and pencil from her cabin below and headed toward the stern of the ship, settling on the bench near Duncan. With a happy sigh, she thought about the new adventure waiting for them on Kauai.

As if he sensed her thoughts, Duncan spoke up from his spot at the wheel. "When we get to Kauai, we'll anchor in Nawiliwili Harbor." He twirled his handlebar moustache and gazed straight ahead at the whitecapped sea. "I'm eager to pick up the trail of me da's last days."

Abby thought about Duncan's father, Ian, who had left Scotland to escape his heartache after his beloved wife had died. Although he'd left Duncan in Scotland with an aunt, the little boy had grown up to become a private detective who had been on his father's trail for years.

Duncan had learned that his father had eventually traveled to the islands and fallen in love with a Hawaiian princess. But there was evidence in the journal Abby had discovered that Ian had met with trouble. At whose hands, and why, they weren't sure. But Duncan intended to find out.

"How are you going to pick up the trail?" Abby asked.

"I'm going to start with the Kauai chief me da's new wife was supposed to marry. Hopefully, that will lead me to Kalele, me da's wife. If I can find her, I might learn about me da."

Kini, with his short-cropped black hair, arrived at the stern of the ship with Sandy trailing at his heels. When he joined Abby on the bench, Sandy yipped for attention. Kini bent down and gathered the yellow puppy onto his lap.

"You make a cute picture," Abby said, opening her journal to a fresh page. "I'm going to draw it." She began outlining Kini's face and shoulders.

"Why you be looking for your father when he be dead?" Kini asked Duncan.

The Scotsman gripped the large wheel more tightly. For a moment he was silent, then he spoke with a thick brogue. "Me da left when I was but a wee laddie. I suppose 'tis me way of making a connection with him, Kini. Therrre's so much I missed. . . ."

Abby knew his brogue always thickened when he felt emotional.

"I was only half yer age, Kini, when me da left. But I still rrremember his promise to me. We'd been walking through our village, and I'd seen a poster of the circus. 'Twas me first time to see an elephant." Duncan winked at Abby and Kini with his one gray eye. "'Daddy,' I said, 'please take me to see the elephants.' But the circus had already come and gone. 'I'll carve ye a wee elephant,' he said when he saw how disappointed I was."

Kini's dark eyes shone with interest. "Do you still have the wee elephant?"

"Nay," Duncan said with a shake of his head. "Me da left right after, and I never heard from him again . . . but for years I hoped he would send me one."

Kini's shoulders drooped. He lifted Sandy to his chin and received several sloppy licks from her quick pink tongue. Then he buried his face in the puppy's neck.

Duncan eyed Abby and nodded for her to take the wheel. She jumped up and gripped the shiny wooden spokes as Duncan sat next to Kini. "Though it was not to be, Kini, the good Lord did send me the wooden dolphin me da carved and

Abby found on Lanai. And best of all, me da's own thoughts that he recorded in his journal."

Kini looked up, searching the Scotsman's kind face, but he remained silent, his mouth drawn into a frown.

"God will not let you down, Kini." Duncan hugged the lonely boy's shoulders.

"Woof!" Sandy barked, as if she agreed. And Kini's lips finally relaxed into a smile.

Chapter Three

Sunup the next day dawned bright and clear. Abby and Luke swabbed the deck as the *Fair Winds* plowed through the swells off the Kauai coastline. Kai stood at the helm.

Duncan sauntered up behind Abby and Luke, a mug of steaming coffee in one hand. He took a sip of the fragrant brew. "Kai says we'll sight the harbor mouth of Nawiliwili soon." The coast they traveled was lush with tropical plants. Duncan shook his head with wonder. "It's as emerald green as the Irish coast I once sailed by," he remarked.

Liho, high in the rigging, suddenly gave a shout of triumph as he sighted the bay. He scurried down the rigging and joined Abby and Luke in reefing down the sails to a quarter of their full size. They would need to reduce speed and move slowly into the harbor.

"Heads up!" Duncan yelled, taking the wheel and steering the vessel into the harbor channel.

As Abby and Luke hurried to the bow to catch a

view of this new place, they noticed a ship barreling toward them at a fast clip. It was a decrepit schooner, with black paint peeling along its side.

"That ship's hogging our lane," Luke growled. "Doesn't the captain know maritime rules about entering and exiting a harbor?"

But the ship came on, full sail, cutting a reckless wake toward them.

Abby stood rooted to the deck. Surely the vessel would turn back into its proper lane.

She could see the white foam at its bow, one sailor busy in the shrouds, another emptying a bucket at the side.

"She's on a collision course with us!" Abby shrieked. Kai hurried to join them. He put a burly fist on Abby's shoulder and peered ahead. Grunting with dissatisfaction, he turned and fled toward the stern, apparently to alert Duncan.

Pa and Uncle Samuel emerged from below the deck. "What's all the commotion?" Uncle Samuel asked. But he and Pa quickly took in the situation.

"Is that captain drunk?" Pa asked angrily. "Ahoy!" he shouted, hoping to alert someone on the other ship to their collision course with the *Fair Winds*.

Duncan inched the ship closer to the channel rocks. "Blazes!" he shouted.

Luke and Abby began hollering at the oncoming vessel. Only a short distance stood between a life-shattering crash! As Abby screamed a warning, the ship kept bearing down on them. *Something about that ship looks familiar,* Abby thought briefly.

At the sound of their frantic shouts, one of the sailors finally looked up. His mouth dropped open, and Abby could hear him yell. At the last possible second, the black ship veered sharply, and its wake punched the *Fair Winds'* hull. Their ship knocked about, and Abby heard dishes crash below the deck. "Ma might need me!" she exclaimed to Luke, hurrying away.

As she started down the hatch, she turned quickly to see the black ship sail on by. A man at the helm, tall and as run-down as his ship, stood at the wheel laughing at their near miss! Abby caught his profile for a split second, then hurried below, thinking, *Who does he remind me of?*

An hour later, they were on their way to the sugar plantation where Olani's cousin lived and worked. The sun beat down on the red dirt road as Abby and her family hiked the three miles inland. Kai and Liho had stayed behind to guard the ship.

Sandy had started out prancing alongside Luke. But now she slowed as the heat and distance wore her out. Abby glanced down. Sandy's little tail was beginning to drag in the dirt. "Know just how you feel, girl." She shouldered her carpetbag and envied Sarah, whom Pa now carried.

But in another half hour, they turned a corner in the road and gaped at the sight that met their eyes: off the main track was a narrower dirt road lined with tall palm trees. The wrought iron gate stood open, and the curling black words above it read, "Cutter Grove Plantation."

"We're here!" Sarah exclaimed.

On each side of the beautiful trees, row upon row of tall sugarcane waved in a fragrant breeze. It was light green and rustled like paper in the wind. "*Ko,*" Kini said. "This be *ko*—sugarcane."

Soon the palms gave way to a wide, plush lawn before a two-story mansion. Bright red and pink flowers bordered the expansive house, which was white with a wraparound *lanai,* or porch. To the left and right of the acre of grass, a grove of giant mango trees shaded the sides of the lawn. Blankets and tables were spread under the trees on the right, with many Hawaiians milling about. It was apparent they had arrived in the middle of a feast, and Abby's nose began to twitch at the delicious aromas.

Duncan and Pa led them toward the Hawaiian crowd, whom Abby guessed were the plantation workers. Many stopped eating to give a friendly nod, but one smiling woman with long dark hair stopped serving food at the table and came forward. Abby immediately wondered if she could be Olani's distant cousin.

The Hawaiian woman's broad face lit up with

kindness. "*Aloha,*" she murmured. "What we can do for you?"

Pa set Sarah down, and he spoke up. "We're looking for someone who works here—a woman named Malama."

"I am Malama!" the woman exclaimed, surprised.

Pa smiled happily. "Olani, from Kailua, sent us. We came to learn about a sugar plantation."

Malama's face softened and she nodded. "Olani!" She beamed at the name and welcomed them without further question. "So, you want to understand this business? Well, first you join us and refresh from your journey. Yes?" Without waiting for an answer, she turned and led them toward the banquet tables.

Once there she introduced them to her husband, Hoku, a robust man with graying temples. He helped Malama seat everyone on blankets, then delivered plates of food to them.

"Look!" Sarah said. "He has a shark necklace just like Kini's."

"Shhh, Sarah," Abby said, leaning toward her sister. "It's not nice to stare." But young children with large brown eyes were staring at them from the edge of the blanket. "*Aloha!*" Abby said, and they giggled behind their hands.

Kini watched them with keen interest while he dipped his fingers in a bowl of purple paste and sucked the gooey *poi* from them. The look of ecstasy as he swallowed made the children laugh again.

Ma turned to Malama, asking, "What are you celebrating?"

Malama answered softly. "This be a funeral feast to honor Naomi, Lani's mother, who served many years here," she explained. "We buried her in Christian burial today." Malama's gaze veered toward a low, distant hill, where a slim woman was heading toward gravestones. Abby could see her long hair swaying past her waist. Her dark brown locks were highlighted in the sun with just a touch of auburn.

"That be Lani," Malama went on. "After long illness, her mother passed into Jesus' waiting arms." Malama wiped her eye quickly. "Naomi was so gentle. She knew the Cutter family the longest. Came when they first started the plantation and served as head housekeeper for many years. When the Cutter parents died six years ago, she served as hostess for the big house, too. Now it be Lani's job." The Hawaiian woman inclined her head toward the mansion, and Abby saw a tall dark-haired man standing on the wraparound porch. Although his face was partially shaded by potted palms, Abby could see that the corners of his mouth turned down.

"Who's that?" she asked, sensing that the man had been watching them since their arrival.

Malama glanced over as the man started down the porch steps. "That be Mr. Cutter—Reese

Cutter—the owner of this plantation." Abby saw the slight scowl on Malama's face and wondered about it.

As Reese Cutter crossed the lawn and drew near the feast, Hoku grimaced.

Mr. Cutter, who appeared younger than Pa, approached the banquet tables and stood with hands behind his back. He was handsome, with a straight nose and strong chin. Dressed in cream-colored trousers and black riding boots, he looked the part of a gentleman farmer. His dark hair and moustache glinted in the sun as he inclined his head toward Hoku. "You've all eaten. It's time now to get back to work," Cutter boomed.

Plantation workers immediately began murmuring, though no one dared to meet his stare. They began gathering and folding blankets. The giggling children dispersed and ran toward the grass huts Abby saw in the distance to the far right of the mansion.

Pa, Duncan, and Uncle Samuel quickly stood up as Reese Cutter strode toward them. "And you are?" he questioned, one dark eyebrow quirked. Introductions were quickly made, and Pa explained that they had come to learn about the sugar trade. Mr. Cutter wasted no time in small talk. "Do you want a job?" he asked. "I've lost many workers to the California gold rush. Seven left just this week."

Behind her, Abby heard Malama's husband mutter, "That not be the only reason."

But Pa must not have heard, for he seemed caught up in the offer. "We'd be glad to help out for a while, but I can't say how long we'll be here."

"That's all right," Reese Cutter said. "You're interested in learning, and I need extra hands." Abby noticed his voice had taken on a warmer quality since Pa and Uncle Samuel accepted the job.

"My father and mother worked hard to build this business out of the wilds," he explained. "Unfortunately, they perished six years ago in a carriage accident. But they always helped those who came to them. I'm happy to extend a friendly hand," he said, shaking hands with Pa and Uncle Samuel.

Duncan cleared his throat. "I won't be working with the Kendalls," he explained, "as I've come to search for information about me da. I have a lead on a Kauai chief who knew him. And I'm looking for the woman my father married many years ago. Her name was Kalele. Have you heard of her?"

Reese Cutter paused, closing his eyes in thought. "No, it doesn't sound familiar, Mr. MacIndou. But I'll tell you what. I can lend you a horse for your journey around the island. I can also lend you a map."

Duncan beamed.

"Why don't you all follow me?" Reese asked. "We have worker huts you can settle in, and then you can join me in the big house for dinner tonight."

Although Reese phrased his suggestion like a question, Abby sensed he expected them to accept.

"I'd like you to meet Lani, my housekeeper," he continued. "She could use the diversion, since her mother has just died. We don't get many visitors here. We're eager for news of the outside world." He smoothed his jet-black moustache and smiled charmingly at Charlotte Kendall.

"What a nice man!" Abby whispered to Luke. Reese was being so kind toward her family and friends. And he was obviously concerned for Lani, his housekeeper.

As Reese Cutter walked away from the native grass shacks that had been left abandoned, Abby and Luke gazed in amazement at each other. The tall grass-walled huts were spacious inside, but they were disasters! The floors were hard-packed dirt, and black bugs crawled about.

Charlotte Kendall held her nose as she exited the one Reese had graciously offered them. "This will take an hour of work to clean out," she lamented. "Thomas, please set our little bit of luggage under that tree. We can't put anything, or anyone, in there until we sweep out all of those bugs!"

Pa cringed. "I'll go see if I can scrounge up a broom for you, Charlotte."

"There's one thing I have to do first, before I get started," Charlotte said, smoothing her skirt and tucking a stray lock of hair back into her bun. "Abby, come with me." She took her daughter's hand, and the two began to walk toward the little cemetery on the hill.

As the hot sun beat down on them, Ma explained. "I feel compelled to offer comfort to Lani. She's just lost her mother, and . . . she looked so lonely walking away."

As they passed through the small white gate and into the shaded graveyard, they saw Lani kneeling by a fresh grave. A lei of pink plumeria blossoms lay on the dirt. Ma and Abby kneeled quietly down a few feet from the housekeeper.

When Lani looked up, Abby instinctively gasped. Lani was stunningly beautiful. Her delicate features reminded Abby of her mother's cameo brooch, but Lani's lovely skin was the color of light, creamed coffee. Yet her most striking feature was her eyes, so different from the dark chocolate of most Hawaiians. Although hers were puffy from crying, they were a dazzling pale blue, like the turquoise water of a shallow bay.

"Lani," Ma began, "I'm Charlotte, and this is my daughter Abby. We came to say we're sorry for your loss. We've just arrived from Oahu. My husband found work here. But if there's anything we can do—please, let us help."

Lani's eyes softened. "*Mahalo,* thank you," she said. "This is a sad day for me, yet I should be happy. I know Mother is in heaven—where there are no more tears. The Lord took care of her for many years. I know He has said, 'Well done, good and faithful servant.'" Lani's eyes pooled with tears. "But I am already so lonely for her."

Ma moved closer and put an arm around her. "Let the tears come, dear," Ma crooned. "It will do you good." She looked at the freshly dug, unmarked earth. "Is there no headstone for the grave?"

Lani sniffed and wiped her tears with the back of one hand. "Yes, it's coming soon. Reese ordered it for me, even though I owe him so much already for doctor bills. . . ."

Ma gently patted Lani's back while Abby smiled sadly. *How kind of Reese. He's been paying the doctor bills all this time,* she thought. *And there's only one reason he'd do that. He must have liked Naomi, and I bet he cares a great deal for Lani!*

Chapter Four

That evening Abby gazed around the sparkling dining room of the big house. Luke, sitting next to her at the long elegant table, leaned close. "These are real rich diggin's," he whispered, glancing at the silver tea service on the sideboard.

Abby grinned at him as a servant cleared her soup bowl away. White linen, a hanging crystal chandelier lit with many candles, silver, and cream-colored china gleaming—it all made her feel like a princess in a palace.

At the head of the table sat Reese Cutter, a handsome and smiling host. At the opposite end sat their regal hostess, Lani, her long, rich hair done up on her head and her blue silk gown accenting her eyes. If Ma felt out of place in her cotton dress, she didn't show it, Abby thought. She was as gracious and well mannered as any lady.

"Kauai is lovely," Ma said as she buttered her roll.

"Yes," Reese agreed, "it's lush and productive. But do keep your eyes open for the *menehune*."

Then with a wink, "They are known to cause mischief at night."

Ma cocked her head. "The *menehune*? Are you speaking of those large insects in our grass house?"

Reese laughed. "No, the *menehune* are the 'little people' of Kauai. Sort of like Irish leprechauns, I'd say."

Lani raised a speculative eyebrow. "We have many ancient fishponds, walls, and aqueducts, all made of stone. Some think the *menehune* built them," she said with a teasing wink, "because the stone creations were here when the first Hawaiians settled on Kauai a thousand years ago."

"Legend has it," Reese explained, "that the *menehune* built them in a night. Of course, it would take us many years to complete such projects. But when the Hawaiians came, the *menehune* vanished into the hills, preferring their privacy."

"But many believe that when mischief occurs, the *menehune* have visited," Lani explained.

Abby looked at Kini and Sarah. Their eyes were huge with excitement. "I'm gonna stay awake all night and wait to catch one!" Sarah said. "Do they have to give you your wish, like a leprechaun does?"

Reese laughed. "No, but I think you could charm them into giving you something, Sarah."

"I know just what I want," she said, glowing with enthusiasm. "I want a birthday party!"

Ma and Pa eyed each other. "That's a family affair, Sarah," Ma said in a firm tone.

34

Reese grinned at Ma. "No, no. It's a good idea. I don't see why we can't have a cake here one night to celebrate." Turning to Sarah, he addressed her kindly, "What day is your birthday, little lady?"

"June 22!"

"Why, that's just two days away," Reese said. He thought briefly. "Come back Thursday night at seven for cake, all right?"

Sarah nodded, then, flushed with excitement, turned to Kini. "A party with cake and games!"

Everyone laughed, and the conversation turned to the plantation and the jobs Pa and Uncle Samuel would begin tomorrow. "Thomas and Samuel," said Reese, "I'm going to send you with Hoku. He's been the overseer for years and knows everything about running this plantation. From the fields to the refinery, Hoku manages everyone. He'll probably put you in the fields and also have you work with the processing machines. Payday is Friday, and you can purchase all you need at the store right here on the plantation."

Luke grinned with anticipation. "Where will I work, Mr. Cutter?"

Ma gave him a reproving look. "Luke, you'll be joining the other children and me. I've heard that there's been no schooling for three months now, and we're going to fix that with the first day of school starting tomorrow morning."

Luke hung his head. "Yes, ma'am."

Lani spoke up gently, her eyes on Luke. "School

is a privilege, Luke. Not everyone has such an opportunity. I was lucky to live in the big house most of my life and learn English from Mrs. Cutter. She was a wonderful teacher."

By ten o'clock in the evening, the four-course meal drew to a close, and Reese Cutter thanked everyone for coming. He laid his white napkin on the table and rose to shake hands with the men. Then he crossed to Lani, put his large hands on her shoulders, and leaned down to speak to her. Lani stiffened at his touch. "Don't do any more work," Abby heard Reese say. "It's been a long day. Why don't you get some rest?"

Lani only smiled briefly. Reese headed out of the dining room, crossing the large parlor, and swept up the grand staircase.

As two servants came in to clear the rest of the table, Lani rose and gathered dishes, too. Ma and Pa thanked her again and began to herd the sleepy children out the front door. Duncan picked up Sarah, and Uncle Samuel carried Kini back to the shack that all the men but Pa shared. But Abby paused. "Ma, can I stay and help Lani clean up? She's had a long day, and I'd like to help."

Ma smiled at Abby. "That's a good idea, dear," she said, pressing a kiss to Abby's forehead. "Then come to bed."

As Abby stepped back into the dining room and began stacking dishes in her arms, Lani gave her a grateful look. "*Mahalo*," she said. "We have a big mess in the kitchen, what with all the cooking for the feast."

She led the way, and Abby quickly saw that Lani had not been exaggerating. Dishes were piled on every counter, pots and pans scattered over the blackened stove, and two servants were putting away food in the huge kitchen. Malama stood with her arms in a sink full of dishes, washing away. Lani handed Abby a towel, and soon the two were drying dishes for Malama.

Malama grinned good-naturedly. "Big mess today, but tomorrow I go back to my job at the company store," she explained. "When we have feasts or dinner guests, I come to the big house to help."

"Mother used to love working side by side with Malama," Lani said sadly. "You two were the best of friends."

"Yes, your sweet mama was wonderful, Lani." Malama turned her head to Abby. "Even when she got sick, she still try to do her work in the big house. But the illness, it wear her down."

Lani said softly, "She hated having anyone wait on her. She liked doing for others."

Malama nodded. "Everyone be Naomi's friend. Even the doctor, that old grouch. He came to love her, too."

"That's wonderful you have a doctor in this area," Abby said as she dried.

Malama spoke up. "Even though the doctor finally become Naomi's friend, he still always charge for his visits and medicines. Now Lani be in debt to that man."

"No," Lani corrected. "I'm in debt to Reese, who paid the bills. . . . It will take years to pay him back."

"Everyone be in debt to that man," Malama spat out. "But he especially be glad Lani be in debt to him."

"Why?" Abby asked, surprised by the change in Malama's voice.

"Oh, he be liking Lani for years now. She just never say yes to him!" Malama said as she handed Abby a dripping plate.

Lani only blushed.

Malama went on. "Six years ago that boy, he be a good catch. But something change since his parents die. Now he make all the money and spend it all on himself. Shame on him!" she said, shaking a soapy finger in the air as if Reese were there. "He should have paid the doctor bills for Naomi just because she be giving her whole life to this plantation. His parents would have."

"Speaking of money," Lani interjected, "did you see the new marble table he had delivered yesterday to the library?"

"No!" Malama scowled and scrubbed a pot harder.

"This is a beautiful home," Abby said, hoping to smooth over Malama's anger.

Lani took the dried dish from Abby. "Would you like a tour of the downstairs when we're done here?"

"Yes!" Abby beamed.

Twenty minutes later, Lani led Abby through the huge pantry with rows of gold-and-pink cans of papaya, star fruit, and mango. On they went through the exquisite dining room, the downstairs parlor with the painting of the Cutter parents, and then the elegant sitting room with a piano. Next Lani took her down the hall and showed her the wood-paneled library, its shelves filled with rare volumes of leather-bound books. Off to the left of the library through some French doors was the attached study. Lani went to close the opened window, through which a deliciously cool breeze now flowed, making the many potted palms wave. In the center of the room sat a large oak desk and chair. Behind it stood a steel vault.

"Wow," Abby enthused, "a real vault to hold valuables!" She strode over, kneeled, and examined it close-up.

"Yes," Lani answered, "and Reese wears the only key for it around his neck."

What could be hidden in the vault so he'd have the only key? Abby wondered as she stood up and passed the desk again. There, on the wide desktop, sat a daguerreotype of an older couple in a gold frame. "Are those Mr. Cutter's parents?" she asked Lani.

"Yes," Lani said lovingly, as she picked up the frame and handed it to Abby.

Abby studied the two handsome people who resembled Reese. "He looks like them both," she said as she leaned over a stack of papers on the desk to replace the daguerreotype. Just before she turned to follow Lani from the room, her eye caught a name scrawled at the bottom of the top sheet of paper: *Captain James Canter! Sugar lumps! That's why the captain of the black ship looked familiar,* she realized. *He's here on Kauai! The very same scoundrel who tossed Luke and me overboard on our way to Lanai! And the one who might be responsible for the disappearance of Duncan's father.*

Her thoughts swirling, Abby followed Lani from Reese's study. She shivered at the thought of encountering Cap'n Jim again. But it was possible they might run into him, if he did business with Reese Cutter.

The tour now finished, Abby and Lani returned to the kitchen. As Malama led the way through the now-clean kitchen, Abby followed and was the last one out the back door. "Shouldn't I lock the door somehow?" Abby asked.

Malama's voice crackled with delight. "Lock? What is that? Here on Kauai, we all be friends! If you need to go in the big house, you just go in."

Even Lani smiled at the idea of locking a door. "I've forgotten things and walked right in late at night," Lani assured her. "Reese has never minded. He usually sleeps right through it. In fact, the only time he ever got upset was when I woke him by accident."

The three headed toward their grass shacks a distance from the still-lit mansion. The farther away they got, the more the night stars glittered like jewels on black velvet. Coconut palms swayed overhead, and the breeze carried the scent of sweet ginger and sugarcane.

"Good night," Malama said as she took a narrow path leading to her own place.

Lani walked Abby to her little hut. "If you need anything," Lani said, "just call. My hut is right next to yours."

"Thanks, Lani. Why don't you live at the big house like you used to?"

"After the Cutter parents died, Mother wanted her own little hut for the two of us. I will continue to stay there."

"Sweet dreams," Abby said softly as she stole through the open doorway of their tall grass hut. Though there were no windows in the hut, Abby could feel a cool breeze coming through the walls, and the sound was soothing. Thank goodness they'd had daylight hours to clean it out, she thought as she slipped into her nightdress under the cover of darkness. Sarah snored gently as Abby settled onto the straw-stuffed ticking on the floor. Ma and Pa were asleep in a rope bed that hung a few inches above the ground.

Abby tugged a little of the sheet out of Sarah's

clutches as she turned on her side. The straw rustled as she moved, but then all grew quiet except for the gentle sound of the grass walls. Abby's mind, however, still spun with questions. How could Reese Cutter, who seemed so nice, have anything to do with Cap'n Jim, who she knew to be a scoundrel? *Just wait 'til I tell Duncan,* she thought.

And why is Malama so angry at Reese? Could it have anything to do with Cap'n Jim, or is it because Reese spends too much money? It seems odd that Malama would care about that when he's such a nice man. Goodness, he even offered to throw a party for Sarah, and we're strangers to him. But he seems especially nice to Lani.

Abby remembered the caring way Reese had touched Lani's shoulders. *If Lani married Reese, she'd be out of debt faster than you can say "sugar lumps,"* she thought.

A sudden scratching noise snapped her out of her reverie. For a few minutes Abby listened. She was so tired, but the noise made her curious. What could it be? Finally she sat up and lit the candle perched on the floor by her bed. The flame hissed for a moment, and Abby picked up the candleholder and held it up high. To her horror, three huge black cockroaches stared back at her from a few feet away. Their antennae twitched in the candlelight. Angry that the bugs had returned after all the hard work, Abby picked up one of her boots and threw it at them. She was mortified when they remained in place, apparently not the least afraid!

"Oh, my!" Abby breathed. She quickly doused the flame, dove back under the covers, and yanked the sheet over her head.

Chapter Five

"I dreamed a huge cockroach ate our grass hut last night!" Abby told Ma with a shudder the next morning.

"I'm disheartened by their return this morning," Ma said as she stabbed the dirt floor with the broom in angry sweeps. A two-inch-long cockroach went flying out the door.

"Ugh!" Sarah screamed, running from the shack. A cockroach flew by her. "I want to live in the big house!"

"Sarah," Ma called out, "you and Luke set up this blanket under the mango trees. We'll start school soon."

Pa and Uncle Samuel had already left for a day of work while the children had slept. Duncan had tipped his hat, Ma now told Abby, and promised to be back in a few days as he'd ridden out on a borrowed horse.

When Abby heard a little *woof* at the door, she

grinned and took off her apron. "Come on, Ma. This dirt floor is as clean as it's going to get. Let's head out."

Ma gathered her Bible and several sheets of paper. "Where'd I put those schoolbooks, Abby?" she asked in an irritated tone. Abby smiled to herself. Ma wasn't the most organized person in the world.

"Under this pile of clothes, Ma," Abby answered as she picked up her slate and two books. Carrying them under her arm, she walked on the edge of the wide lawn and arrived at the blanket, where the feast had been the day before. Sarah had found a wilted plumeria lei, which she sweetly draped over Ma's shoulders with a hug.

Kini, Luke, Abby, and Sarah sat down on the blanket in front of Ma, who opened to the Gospel of Luke and began their daily reading. "'No servant can serve two masters . . . ,'" she read. "'You cannot serve both God and Money.'" Abby noticed that Luke nodded in agreement as he played with Sandy, who sat in his lap.

"I learned that lesson," Luke said, "when I got a bad case of gold fever. Caring more about money than God will make you crazy. You'll do stupid things."

Abby gazed proudly at Luke, who'd finally chosen to follow God in the California wilderness when a grizzly bear almost killed him. The bear had gotten Sparks, Luke's beloved dog of many years, instead. Although Luke still grieved his loss, Abby could see Luke's hunger to learn more about Jesus and the Bible.

A few minutes later, Lani came by dressed in a long skirt and white blouse, ready for a day of work at the big house. Swinging a basket on one arm, she stopped at their blanket. Abby could smell freshly baked bread.

"Morning, everyone," Lani said, setting down the basket. "I brought you some Hawaiian sweet bread and fresh vegetables from my garden. Charlotte, be sure to see Malama at the store today and put anything you need on a bill. They'll take out what you owe from Thomas's paycheck at the end of the week."

"Why, thank you," Ma exclaimed as Lani headed off with a wave.

Lani reminded Abby of the Bible verse Ma had finished with: *Do not be deceived, God is not mocked; for whatever a man sows, this he will also reap.* Lani had sowed kindness, and she was already reaping their friendship.

Two hours later, school was done for the day. "I think I'll break you kids in easy," Ma teased. "Abby and Luke, would you take this list I've written up to the store and get what we need?"

"Sure thing," Luke said, hopping up. He reached a hand down to help Abby up, and the two were off.

"Ma," Abby heard Sarah whine as they crossed the lawn, "Kini and I want to go to the store, too."

"But I need you two for a very important chore," Ma said. "You must stay here and keep Sandy out of mischief for me."

As they entered the cool interior of the Plantation Store, as it was named on the sign, Malama glanced up from her place behind the counter. *"Aloha,"* she greeted them. "It's my little dish drier."

Abby grinned as Luke handed her the list of groceries Ma wanted.

"Your mother needs flour and sugar," Malama said, loading things into the basket Lani had left them. She referred back to the list as she pulled things off the well-stocked shelves. Soon the basket was loaded high.

"I wonder how much all this will cost," Luke commented as he picked up the heavy basket.

"Plenty, you can be sure." Malama shook her head. "Mr. Reese, he only pay workers in scrip, too."

"What's *scrip?*" Abby asked. She'd never heard the word before.

"Ah, it be a little piece of paper he makes here at

the plantation. It's like money, but the only place
you can spend it is here at the store. And everything
here costs too much!"

"That's not fair!" Abby said.

"No, it not be fair. But he's the boss. When his
parents were alive, they never did this. But that was
six years ago. Lots can change in six years."

Luke growled. "If you have to spend your pay
here, that means he's making even more money off
his workers. Especially if the prices are too high."

Malama's wide face scowled. "That be the truth.
No one gets ahead here. Most of my friends, they go
in debt more and more 'cause Mr. Cutter keeps
raising the prices."

"Are we talking about the same Mr. Cutter who
was so nice to us last night?" Abby asked, puzzled.
"He seems like such a caring person."

Malama snorted. "*Humph.* He be nice when it
help him get what he wants."

The bell over the door jangled as Kini and Sarah
came in. "Ma says I can buy some peppermints!"
she announced. Sandy was on a string leash at her
heels.

Malama grinned, her frustration no longer show-
ing. "We have rock candy, *keiki*. But you don't need
peppermints here. This be a sugar plantation." The
big woman opened the door, leaned out, and spoke
in Hawaiian to some young children who were
playing nearby.

When a boy came in, Malama said, "Ono, take

these nice *haoles* to the field and show them how to pick some candy." Sarah's eyes fairly danced with anticipation as they trooped behind Ono and three other children into the tall, rustling cane.

"Imagine, candy growing right outside," Sarah exclaimed. Ono took out a pocketknife, cut a long length of cane, then chopped it into pieces for everyone. They each followed his lead, peeling back the outer husk and sucking on the sugary meat inside.

Kini smiled blissfully. "It be warm and sweet!"

Abby turned to Ono. "Why aren't you in school?"

He looked confused. "No school no more. A long time ago, Mama said they have school here. But the school—it be closed now."

Sarah stopped sucking long enough to pipe up, "My ma is the best teacher anywhere. You can come to our school." She pointed to the mango grove. "We meet over there every morning."

Ono's eyes met Abby's. "Could we?"

"Of course," Abby said. "Ma will be glad to help out."

The children broke into shy smiles. *"Mahalo,"* Ono said. "We be there."

As Abby and the others headed back toward their own hut with the supplies, Luke seemed unusually quiet.

"A penny for your thoughts," Abby teased. "What are you thinking about?"

"Just wondering why the plantation school was

closed," he murmured as he pushed his straight hair off his forehead. He looked troubled.

Abby glanced back at the Hawaiian children still sitting on the store porch, looking bored. "There must be a good reason," she said, her forehead wrinkling. "I just can't think of one."

Chapter Six

Abby stirred the savory pot of stew over the open fire pit. The sun was setting in the west, and the trade winds shook the nearby cane and sweet-smelling plumeria trees.

Ma was busy setting out chipped bowls on a blanket for dinner. Uncle Samuel and Pa were reclining on *tapa* mats in the nearby shade. Their faces were sunburned, and they seemed weary after their 12-hour workday. But Uncle Samuel, who had been sick many months before, now looked healthy and strong again.

"I tell you, Abby," he said excitedly, "now I know why Kauai is called the 'Garden Isle.' The moisture, rich soil, hot sun—it all makes for perfect growing conditions. And the insect life!" He sat up. "I've never seen such large critters. Spiders in the cane fields are a lovely green and yellow." He opened his fist and splayed his fingers. "Almost as big as my hand!"

"No!" Abby shuddered. *That* would be her worst

nightmare. For heaven's sake, the cane fields were all around the plantation grounds! What if a spider got into their hut one night?

"Well, I might be exaggerating just a little," Uncle Samuel said, chuckling, "but they *are* giant sized."

Luke grinned at her. "Why don't we catch a few and set 'em loose in the shacks to eat the cock-roaches?"

"No you don't, Luke Quiggley!" Abby fumed. "They could carry off Sandy!" She bent down and patted the sleeping pup.

Luke's mischievous eyes crinkled at the corners. "Just an idea, Abby."

Everyone around the fire pit laughed at Abby's fear of spiders. But she good-naturedly dished up stew for all, insisting that Ma sit down and Sarah deliver the steaming bowls.

After dinner Abby and Sarah made cinnamon tarts from pie dough, frying them over the fire in a little grease. The sugar and cinnamon soon bubbled into a gooey syrup that made a sticky-sweet dessert.

Later Abby stood soaping dishes in a large tin tub while Luke dried beside her. Both looked up when Lani walked by on her way home from work at the big house. Her head hung down, as if she was either tired or sad. Even so, she was beautiful with her long, silky hair swaying below her waist. Abby wiped her hands on her flour-sack apron and set a few leftover tarts on a pie plate.

"Come on, Luke," she said, noting that Sarah and

Kini were busy playing *konane*, the Hawaiian rock game that was so similar to checkers. "Let's go take these over to Lani."

Luke jumped up, Sandy tagging along at his heels. They intercepted Lani just as she reached her door.

"These are for you," Abby said, handing Lani the tin of cinnamon tarts.

"*Mahalo*. Come in, please," she said with a kind smile.

The hut was darkly shadowed, but Abby could see a double bed, two chairs and a table, and an armoire for clothes. Lani crossed the earthen floor and lit a lantern, which sat on the table. Now that the room was bright and cheery, Abby noticed the brilliant red-and-white quilt across the bed.

"This is beautiful," she said, walking toward the bed and touching the quilt.

"My mother made it many years ago," Lani said, sounding pleased. "It's the Hawaiian wave pattern."

Abby studied the bold red pattern waving out from the center of the quilt to its corners.

"Just looking at it makes me miss her more," Lani said sadly.

"Tell us about her," Abby urged.

When Lani motioned for them to sit down, she and Luke sat across from her on the bed.

For a moment Lani traced a piece of red patchwork reverently with one finger. Then she gazed up at them, her eyes bright with tears. "When my mother was pregnant with me, my father was lost at sea. But she never stopped loving him. Through all these years, no one has taken his place. After he died, she came to work for the Cutters. I was born here on the plantation." Lani paused, drew a breath, and then continued. "She named me 'Lani,' which means 'sky.' She said my eyes were sky blue like my father's."

"How romantic," Abby gushed.

Luke rolled his eyes. Abby could see he was almost ready to bolt out the door.

"After all these years, Mother is finally reunited with him . . . and at home with the Savior she loved. She must be so happy." Lani retrieved a box of clothing from under the bed. She handed Abby a pair of leather sandals. "Could you use these? They were Mother's. She had small feet."

"Yes, thank you," Abby said, grateful to have a cool pair of shoes to slip on instead of her high-laced boots that required stockings.

"Perhaps Charlotte could go through the rest of these clothes," Lani suggested. "Mother's only regret, she said, was leaving me alone. Especially since there are so many doctor bills to pay off." Lani's lip quivered, but she quickly bent down to tuck the box back under the bed. Sandy trotted away from Luke's feet and attacked the side of the box. When she growled and barked at it, Lani laughed.

"I need a friend like you, little pup." She rubbed

Sandy behind an ear, and the puppy wriggled happily, eager for more attention.

"Won't Mr. Cutter forgive all those debts?" Luke asked. "It looks like he has plenty of money."

Lani sighed. "I'm afraid there's only one way he'd do that—if I marry him."

Abby's eyes widened. "Has he *asked* you to marry him?"

Luke groaned and stood up with Sandy in his arms.

"Yes," Lani answered. "But I . . . I cannot."

"Smart decision," Luke mumbled. "Well, Abby, we better get back before your ma misses us."

Lani rose and walked them to the door. "Thank you for the tarts and for listening," she said.

"Aloha," Abby replied, gently reaching out to embrace Lani. How she wished they had been able to do more! "Oh, Lani, thanks for the vegetables today. We put them in a stew for dinner."

Luke cleared his throat. "I have to stick around here for school, but I like to work, Lani. If you need help in your garden, I'm available."

Lani grinned. *"Mahalo!* How about tomorrow?"

"Sure thing," Luke said. "I'll come by in the afternoon."

"Good night." *Lani seems happier now,* Abby thought.

As Luke led the way back to their nearby fire pit, he groused, "There's something I don't like about that Mr. Cutter. He's holding Lani's bills over her head. But if he likes her enough to marry her, why doesn't he like her enough to forget the bills?" His hand swept the surrounding buildings, worker huts, expanse of sugarcane, plush lawn, and well-lit mansion. "Especially when he's got all this?"

Caught up in thinking about Lani, Abby stopped walking while Luke pressed on. She turned and viewed the bright mansion, complete with servants and rooms filled with treasures. And then there was that vault with the single key.

"Good night!" she heard Luke call as he headed to his own hut and disappeared.

Only then did Abby realize she'd forgotten to tell Luke about seeing Cap'n Jim's name in Reese's study. *Surely there's a simple explanation for that,* she told herself, *but what could it be?*

The next morning Sarah woke bright and early. Abby heard her, groaned, and raised her head to look sleepily at her energetic sister.

"Rise and shine, Ma. It's an important day," Sarah called, climbing into her parents' tiny bed.

Ma reached over and gave her a hug. But Pa frowned. "An important day?" he teased. "Ah yes, it's the day we start delivering sugar and molasses to the dock, right?"

Sarah frowned. "No, Pa! It's important 'cause

this is the day your favoritest daughter was born nine years ago!"

Pa rubbed his unshaven whiskers and appeared to give the statement serious thought. "I didn't know Abby was so young. . . ."

Sarah let out a battle cry and attacked him with a pillow, and the fight was on. Abby took her own pillow and attacked Pa, too, just for good measure, and Ma joined the girls. Pa held his own, but before long he let Sarah win the battle.

"To the victor," he announced, "goes the privilege of ordering breakfast for all of us. Madame," he said bowing to Sarah, "what will you have? Eggs, flapjacks, or fried cockroach?"

Sarah giggled and ordered flapjacks with syrup for her birthday breakfast. Luke and Kini arrived shortly to give Sarah a birthday hug. Then everyone scurried about to clean the dishes while Pa and Uncle Samuel grabbed lunches for later in the fields.

When the dishes were done, school began under the shade of the mango trees.

Ma was in the midst of a geography lesson when four Hawaiian children approached timidly.

"Word is spreading that you've started a school," Luke teased. But Ma looked pleased to have more children to teach.

"Come, sit here." She motioned the four children to one side of the blanket as Sarah and Kini moved over a bit. "Abby, I'm going to do a review of basics right now, so why don't you go to the store and see if Malama has any more paper and pencils for our new students?"

"I'll help," Luke said, jumping up. He and Abby hurried off, glad for the recess.

As they climbed the boardwalk in front of the company store, they met Malama coming out. "Oh, you *keikis* startled me!" She gazed affectionately at them. "What you need? I get it quick before I close the store for a while."

"Pencils and paper for our new students," Luke answered. "Some of the kids from the plantation."

"Why are you closing early, Malama?" Abby asked.

She led the way back into the cool store. "Oh, when company expected at the big house, I go help. Tonight I make a special cake for guests who come." She winked, and Abby knew she was talking about Sarah's birthday cake. Then Malama headed behind the counter and bent down while still speaking. "Tomorrow that captain be coming, the one I don't like. He be bad for Mr. Reese."

"What do you mean?" Abby questioned.

Malama straightened and held out eight pencils. "This be the last of them."

Abby took the pencils and pocketed them in her skirt. "Why is that captain a bad influence?"

"Oh, before Mr. and Mrs. Cutter died, that bad man show up here. He want the shipping rights to the sugar, to deliver it to Honolulu. But old Mr. Cutter, he send him away. He didn't like him." She disappeared from view again, searching for paper on the shelf below.

"But when the Cutter parents die, that man show up again. And this time Mr. Reese, he go into business with him. And that's when things start to change."

"What things?" Luke asked.

Malama's head popped up. "He no longer pay us money, but he make up that scrip so we have to buy everything here." She raised herself from a squat and plopped several sheets of paper on the counter.

Abby gathered up the paper, and Malama walked them to the door. "Back then," she went on to explain, "I be very close to Mrs. Cutter." Malama heaved a deep sigh. "That woman be Hawaiian in heart. She be pure gold with much *aloha*. She tell me, 'Malama, when we die, we leave something special for all the workers, and Mr. Reese can finally go traveling like he want.' I think she meant the workers would run the plantation when Mr. Reese travels. And maybe we get a share of the profits."

Abby and Luke watched Malama's face grow stern. "But when Mr. Reese show us the will, it be different. It say they leave the plantation only to him. There be no special gift, like Mrs. Cutter said. It's a mystery because she was great Christian woman, with *aloha* in her heart." She shook her head in dismay.

Luke cleared his throat. "It would be unusual for parents to not leave the land to their son, wouldn't it?"

"Yes, but the Cutters, they love Hawaiians. And they see too many lose their lands to the foreigners that come now. Plus, they know Mr. Reese real good. They know he never like this business. I know they leave him big fortune in money."

She paused before shutting the door behind her. "I think they know Mr. Reese will never be happy here."

"Then why does he stay?" Abby asked, remembering it had already been six years since his parents' deaths.

Malama shrugged and tugged the door closed. "It be easy life for him, and he make much money. But to do it, he almost turn my people into slaves."

Abby's heart picked up speed at Malama's words. "Was it Mr. Reese who shut down the school?"

"Yes, it be him. He say the parents should work, not teach school. And the older *keikis* should help parents in fields." Malama smiled at them sadly. "Sometime, life not be fair. But you help out the littlest ones at your mother's school?"

When Abby nodded, Malama squeezed her tightly. *"Mahalo, keiki.* Tell Charlotte *'mahalo nui loa'* for me." She walked off toward the big house, her lavender muumuu swaying with each step.

As soon as she was sure Malama could no longer hear her, Abby turned to Luke, her cornflower blue eyes blazing with indignation. "So, Reese Cutter closed the school!"

"And for no good reason," Luke said, scowling, "except that he's money hungry. People take stupid risks for the love of money. I should know."

Abby cocked her head. "I don't see him taking any risks."

"He's risked his lifelong friendship with Malama," Luke countered. "And Lani's not too eager to marry him."

Suddenly Abby remembered what she'd seen in Reese's study. "Luke, I forgot to tell you—I saw a business paper in Reese's study with Cap'n Jim's name on it!"

"Jim Canter, the rat who threw us off the ship?"

"The same," Abby said.

"If Reese Cutter is tied up with Cap'n Jim, then he's probably taking lots of risks!"

Abby's eyes darkened. "You don't think he risked changing his parents' will, do you?"

"I think," Luke said softly, "we should investigate that idea. If Canter's involved, we might even find information that leads to Duncan's father."

"You're right," Abby said. "I think we should start by looking in Reese's study, where I saw Cap'n Jim's paper."

"The only question is, how do we get in?"

"Oh, that's easy," Abby said. "All the doors are

left open. Lani told me Reese doesn't mind people coming in at night, so long as they don't wake him."

"We'll have to be careful," Luke said sagely. "You know the old saying about letting sleeping dogs lie."

Chapter Seven

"Abby," Ma said as she stirred a pot of beans over the open fire, "please take Sarah and Kini down to the mango grove and keep them busy this afternoon for me. Maybe you could play Kini's game of *konane*. I have something to do for Sarah's birthday, and I don't want her to see."

"But, Ma, I was going to help Luke weed Lani's garden." Abby brushed a stray ringlet off her face with a floured finger. She was punching down a loaf of homemade bread for dinner.

"I'm sorry, honey. But this is important. You can help Lani another time." Ma untied her apron and hung it on a nearby bush. "I've just got to get this done before tonight."

Abby punched the loaf an extra few times in frustration, then set it in a pan near the fire and covered it with a dishcloth. Hopefully, no bugs would lift the towel and take a bite.

She washed her hands in a bucket of water and called Sarah and Kini. "Let's tell Luke he has to go to Lani's garden without me." They all traipsed off together, Sarah bubbling with excitement about the upcoming party at Reese's big house.

"Ready?" Luke asked as they arrived at his hut. He was barefoot and had borrowed an old straw hat from Hoku to keep the sun off his head as he worked.

"Ma asked me to baby-sit. I'm sorry. You're going to have to work alone."

"It's all right. It's just weeding and hoeing," Luke responded. "I'll probably be done in an hour or two. See you tonight for the party." He winked at Sarah, then headed out toward the spot beyond the cemetery that Lani had showed him.

Sandy tagged along at his heels, nipping them for fun. Just as Abby was about to turn and head the other direction, Luke called out to her. "As long as you're baby-sitting, can you watch Sandy for me? She's going to get in my way and might eat Lani's plants."

Kini ran to Luke and picked up the pup. "Sure, Luke. We watch her good."

Luke hiked off, whistling, and Abby headed in the other direction with Sarah, Kini, and the dog. As soon as they reached the grove, Sarah set up the *konane* game, and she and Kini were quickly engrossed. Abby played with Sandy, tossing a stick over and over. In a while, the puppy grew tired of the game and wandered across the dirt road toward the sugarcane.

"Oh no, you don't," Abby cautioned. She whistled sharply, and the puppy's head came up from sniffing. "Good girl," Abby said when Sandy bounded back to her side. "Sit down and rest."

Sandy curled up beside Abby's leg and promptly fell asleep. As she watched the silver green stalks of sugarcane wave in the late-afternoon breeze, the lazy heat of the island lulled her into a deep relaxation. She lay back on the lawn. Sarah and Kini were happily occupied, and she knew it would be all right to take a little nap.

The first thing Abby heard when she woke was the sound of rustling sugarcane. The wind had picked up noticeably. Abby rubbed her eyes. Sarah and Kini were still engrossed in their game. But where was Sandy?

Hurriedly, she stood up and whistled. "Here, girl!"

Sarah's head turned. "What's wrong?"

"Sandy's missing," Abby said, irritated. "Didn't you notice her wandering off?"

"No, I thought *you* were watching her," Sarah responded. "Besides, it's *my birthday*. I shouldn't have to work today."

Abby clenched her teeth and swallowed her words. After all, it *was* Sarah's birthday.

Kini stood up, his face worried. "We help you look."

"Thanks, Kini. You and Sarah stay put, so no one else gets lost. I think I know where Sandy's gone."

Abby searched the immediate area, calling Sandy's name. But in her heart, she knew where the puppy had disappeared. Into the sugarcane. Sandy had been highly interested in it, and that's where Abby was going to have to look.

But she didn't want to.

Uncle Samuel had said there were cane spiders the size of dinner plates in there. And the cane was much taller than her head. A spider would only have to drop from the top of a stalk to land on her hair. She shuddered at the thought. *Why do I always have to be the one to baby-sit?* she asked herself.

She'd reached the dirt road and was eyeing the spot Sandy had been investigating. Taking a big breath for courage, she plunged in. "Here, Sandy!" she called, pushing cane stalks aside with her hands. "Here, puppy!"

The rows were wide enough to walk down, just barely. Abby could imagine the puppy trotting happily along what would be a wide path to her, oblivious of the lurking, bloodsucking spiders over-head. "Spiders," Uncle Samuel had said, "are excellent predators who bite with fangs and suck out their prey's insides."

Abby was 50 feet into the cane field by now. The memory of Uncle Samuel's words made her want to scream and run. Her skin was crawling with fear, but she had to find Sandy for Luke. "Here, Sandy," she called, this time more softly. No sense in waking up sleeping spiders.

"It's no use. You must be somewhere else, you stupid dog." Abby was truly irritated now and becoming worried. Where could the puppy have wandered off to? She turned around and was about to step forward when a giant spider flew toward her face.

"Ahhhh!" Green legs and a fat, yellow-splashed body flashed across Abby's field of vision. Something touched her hair, and chills raced up her spine and arms. "Help!" she screamed and began to run as fast as her legs could carry her. As she ran, she flailed her arms wildly in an attempt to knock the monster off her head.

Through a break in the cane, she could see the road up ahead. Bursting through the last of the cane field, she pounded across the road, her arms still flailing and screams still erupting from her throat.

Kini and Sarah leapt up at the sight, mouths gaping. By this time, Abby's braid had been completely knocked loose. Her hair was wild and tangled. "Get it out of my hair!" Abby screamed.

But Sarah was laughing so hard at her red-faced sister that it looked as if she could barely breathe.

Kini rushed toward her valiantly and brushed through her hair. "Check my back," Abby ordered.

He searched behind her. "I see nothing, Abby. What you be looking for?"

Abby threw herself onto the grass and almost wept with relief. "Giant killer spiders."

Sarah burst into a new set of hysterical giggles, and Kini joined in.

Abby buried her face in her hands but screamed again when something touched her forehead. She jumped back and saw Sandy standing before her on short puppy legs, trying to lick the salt from her forehead. Sandy's little tail flicked back and forth as quickly as a metronome on a piano.

"You naughty rascal," Abby said, lifting the fluffy ball of fur into her arms. "Don't you know I risked my *life* to find you?"

Abby wished they'd all forget about her experience in the cane field, but it seemed to be everyone's favorite topic over dinner that evening. Uncle Samuel and Pa were in hysterics at Sarah's re-creation of Abby emerging from the sugarcane.

After dinner Uncle Samuel patted her on the back and leaned close. "I had one drop on my shoulder yesterday, Abby," Uncle Samuel confided to her.

Abby gasped. "What did you do?"

"Oh, I just brushed it off. They're pretty puny

compared to us, honey." He looked at her with tenderness in his eyes. "But I understand they give some people the creeps. I get sweaty palms over snakes and heights."

"I think you're brave to go back into the cane fields every day. But I don't understand why God made those awful creatures, Uncle Samuel."

"Sweetheart, that's why I love to study this wide world our Creator made. There's a reason for everything He did, and it's fun to discover it. Now spiders are easy to figure out. They're kind of the wolves of the insect world. If we didn't have them, we'd be overrun with so many other bugs there'd be no room for us humans to sit down."

Abby shivered at that vision.

"Remember, Abby, even the spiders play their part in God's plan. They remind me of other predators, like the evil ones who prey on innocent or weak people. Did you ever wonder why God allows some evil people to keep on living?"

He had her full attention now.

"Yes, I've wondered that. God has all the power in the world. Why doesn't He just get rid of the bad people—like Boris Rassmassen, who got your ranch?"

Uncle Samuel rubbed his hands together, warming up to the talk. "They must play a part in God's plan, too, Abby. Think about it. They show us what evil looks like, then the rest of us get an opportunity to make a choice. Are we going to follow in their ways, or are we going to choose God's way?"

"I never thought of it like that before. I know in the Bible God says, 'Choose life.' So I guess He wants us to choose good things, not the kind of things that bring death."

"Right," Uncle Samuel agreed. "And He wants us to choose the way that leads to eternal life."

Ma emerged from the hut just then, looking lovely in her best yellow calico dress with abalone buttons. Her hair was piled high on her head in a bun, and she looked fresh and pretty. Abby noted that she carried a small brown-papered package in her hand. "Time to go," she said lightly, her eyes gleaming like Sarah's. "We don't want to be late for cake and tea at the big house." At that moment, Abby realized there was a lot of Ma in Sarah.

Sarah came out next, looking thrilled that the time had finally arrived. "Do I look older, Abby?" she asked.

Abby leaned back, studying her. "Yes, you do. After all, you're a girl who's traveled thousands of miles without her parents. I'd say you're pretty mature for a nine year old."

Sarah smiled happily and took Abby's hand as they walked toward the big house. Pa and Ma strolled together, also holding hands. Kini, Luke, and Uncle Samuel, each one cleaned and combed, strode ahead, telling jokes. "Hey, Abby," Luke said, turning to wait for her and Sarah, "I heard a good one while I was working in the garden today with Lani."

Abby and Sarah caught up as Luke began. "What did the melon say to the marriage proposal from the squash?"

Sarah grinned, waiting for the answer.

"I'm too young. I can't elope—get it? Cantaloupe!"

Even Uncle Samuel chuckled.

As they all climbed the porch steps to the big house, Lani opened the screen door. "Welcome, and happy birthday, Sarah."

They were ushered into the dining room right away, where the table was set again with elegant dishes. In the middle of the dining table sat a three-layer white cake beautifully decorated with real flowers. There was punch made of guava and pineapple juices and tea as well. Sarah's eyes brightened when she spied two tiny packages wrapped in banana leaves.

"Come in, come in," Hoku said. "We sit down and wait for the boss. Then," he said with a grin at Sarah, "we eat your cake!"

Malama came through the swinging doors from the kitchen and smoothed her long hair. "I am glad Mr. Reese invited us to come. It has been a long time since we be in this beautiful old house as guests for a party."

When everyone was seated, Reese made his entrance, dressed immaculately in a dark blue suit and fashionable shoes. As he stood at the head of the table, he made a slight bow to Sarah. "Happy birthday," he said simply. "Now, let's enjoy your cake."

Sarah beamed with joy. The cake was sliced and plates served by a servant. Another poured juice. "My, this is special," Ma said to Reese and Lani. "Thank you for making it such a wonderful treat for Sarah."

As soon as the cake was finished and plates cleared, Lani passed Sarah one of the leaf-wrapped gifts. Sarah tore off the bit of string and grinned at the tortoiseshell comb in her hand. "Thank you, Lani!" She immediately set it in her hair where Ma had pulled a section up.

The other gift was from Malama and Hoku. "I always want a child of my own," Malama said simply. "But it was not to be. But I still be loving the *keikis* God brings my way."

Hoku reached out and covered her hand with his thick palm, patting it gently.

Sarah opened the green leaf and squealed with delight as she lifted a white shell necklace from it.

"Those are *puka* shells from a beach near here," Malama explained.

"Thank you," Sarah said excitedly.

Kini volunteered to hook it behind Sarah's neck. Hoku caught his eye and smiled at his helpfulness.

Then Ma passed down the paper-wrapped gift from her and Pa. Inside was a hand-sewn doll with blue eyes and yellow yarn hair. "She looks like me," Sarah said. "I love her, Ma."

Finally, Uncle Samuel addressed Sarah shyly. "I found this today, Sarah. You can start your own collection, since I had to leave mine behind on Oahu."

Sarah oohed as Uncle Samuel held out a tiny bird's nest that had been abandoned. "It's small," she said. "Let's collect a lot, Uncle Samuel, and we'll label them just like yours were."

When everyone got up to leave, Abby noticed Hoku speaking to Kini. They both looked serious and intense. Curiosity got the best of her, and she edged a bit closer. She heard Hoku say, "I miss my father and mother, too. They left many years ago for another island, and I have not seen them since." Hoku patted Kini's back as they moved toward the parlor.

Abby turned away, sad that Kini had apparently mentioned missing his parents, even during a party. How she wished she could change things for him! He'd made a big sacrifice to rescue her and Luke. And there was no going back, she knew. But she remembered how kind Kini's mother had been. No wonder he was suffering.

"Well," Luke whispered to her, as the evening came to a close and people headed toward the front door, "are you ready for our investigation later?"

Before Abby could answer, she caught Reese's eye. He had moved toward them suddenly, as if he were straining to listen. But had he heard?

"Sweet dreams," Lani called as the Kendalls and

company left by the front door. She wouldn't let Luke and Abby help clean dishes, though they had offered to help. "When it's my birthday you may help, but not tonight."

Soon they were all back at their own huts and preparing for bed.

In spite of the company of cockroaches, Abby was learning that grass shacks are wonderful places to live. Island breezes blow through the grass and keep the occupants cool, but at the same time dry from sudden showers—and Kauai seemed to have many brief showers.

As she exited the grass hut in the dark, she was careful not to wake Ma or Pa. She would meet Luke close to the mansion. Then, together, hidden in the nearby grove of mango trees, they'd wait for all the lights of the mansion to blink off.

As she headed quietly across the grass, the fragrance of plumeria blossoms swept over her. She could see that lights were on in a few of the upstairs rooms as she stepped into the deep shadows beneath the trees.

Dry leaves rustled under the new sandals Lani had given her, and Abby came to a halt. It was eerie being all alone in the dark. "Luke," she whispered urgently.

When a hand clamped over her mouth, Abby's eyes widened.

Luke said softly in her ear, "Shhh! We have to be as quiet as possible." When he removed his hand, she twirled to face him.

"Don't do that again! My heart almost stopped." She hoped he couldn't hear it cantering like horse hooves against her ribs.

Luke flashed a grin. "Sorry, peaches. I forgot you bruise easy."

"*Humph.*" Abby turned away, arms crossed, and stared at the house in silence. Within a few minutes, all of the upstairs lights were extinguished.

"It's time," Luke said.

After her fright, Abby wasn't sure she wanted to go tripping through Reese Cutter's lavish home in the dark. The idea had sounded so good during the day, but what if someone thought they were burglars and came down with a loaded gun? What if Reese discovered them? Ma and Pa would hang their heads in shame.

She turned to Luke. "We *can't* get caught."

Luke tweaked her upturned nose playfully. "Don't worry. We'll be out in a jiffy. Don't you want to find out what's going on? And maybe even help out Malama and the others?" He held up a candle he'd brought along. "Let's go."

She swallowed and followed him along the row of trees and around the back of the house to the kitchen steps. They climbed stealthily and turned the knob. As Malama had said, like all the homes on the islands, it was left unlocked.

Luke set the candle down and dug for matches in his pants' pocket. The flame flared and then sputtered on the candlewick. Holding the candle aloft, he led the way through the kitchen and dining room. From there, Abby took the candle and retraced her steps down the hall to the library and adjoining study.

The house was quiet except for an occasional creak and groan of wood cooling from the sun's heat. Abby headed toward Reese's desk. *Best to get this over with quickly,* she thought. Setting the candle on top, she began searching through the desk's many upper compartments.

Luke opened the drawers below and held up documents and various papers to the light. After a few minutes, she heard him sigh. "These are mostly receipts and bills." He sounded disappointed.

Abby, too, had found nothing so far. She opened the final compartment, a drawer directly under the center of the desk. The first few papers appeared to be old letters to the Cutter parents from friends. But suddenly Abby's fingers touched a rolled-up piece of paper tied with a cord. *That's odd,* she thought. *I wonder what it is?* Abby removed the paper and tugged at the cord. *Last Will and Testament,* she read silently.

"Luke, this is it!" she whispered excitedly.

Together they scanned the one-page document.

Abby sighed in frustration. "This is just like Malama said—everything has been left to Reese."

But as she read ahead of Luke to the bottom of the page, she gasped.

"What?" he asked.

"The person who signed this will as a witness is none other than James Canter."

Luke grabbed the paper and stared at the signature. "That scoundrel. Remember how he made us swim a half mile to shore? He must be the captain Malama doesn't like. Now I see her point."

Abby could see the hulking, bowlegged captain in her mind. . . . She hated the way he smelled of garlic, the way he'd laughed when he'd booted them overboard to swim so far to shore. "It's a small world to have run into him again. . . . But Malama said the Cutter parents didn't like him either. So why would they ask him to witness their will?"

"It doesn't add up," Luke agreed. "But if Cap'n Jim is involved in this, I'm sure that something's sour at this sugar plantation."

Abby's eyebrows furrowed. "This means that Cap'n Jim is the one who's been the bad influence on Reese Cutter," she added.

Luke handed her the will.

"Duncan suspects Cap'n Jim had something to do with his father's death . . . ," Abby said slowly.

They digested the thought in silence. Then a bump sounded upstairs! Abby's eyes grew round as they flitted to the open doorway. Luke blew out the candle as Abby shoved the will to the back of the drawer and shut it. They hurried to the door, only to see a candle flame flickering in the upstairs hallway. Abby almost cried out in dismay, but Luke grabbed her hand and pulled her through the lower hall and entryway.

As she looked up, she saw the candle flame bobbing toward the stairs but couldn't make out who was holding it. They rushed through the parlor, then past the dining room and into the kitchen.

She opened the back door and hurried onto the porch as Luke paused for a split second to close the door soundlessly. Then they scrambled down the steps and into the nearest stand of trees, where the shadows were dark and dense.

Her heart thundering, Abby clung to Luke's hand as he led the way back, skirting the open path so no one could see them. While she followed, a memory hovered in the dim recesses of her mind . . . it was important, but she couldn't quite see it. Until Luke made a sudden stop. As she crashed into him, the memory flooded her mind.

"I knew it looked familiar!" she gasped.

"What?" Luke turned to face her.

"The black ship that almost crashed into ours in Nawiliwili Harbor—peeling paint, decrepit, reckless . . ."

Luke grimaced. "The *Beauty*! I should have known it was Cap'n Jim." They hurried back toward their huts, minds churning with this new information.

It was only when Luke said good night at Abby's door and headed toward his own that he remembered he'd left the half-burned candle on the desk.

Chapter Eight

"Last day of school this week," Sarah gushed.

Ma grinned from her spot on the blanket. She closed the reading book with a loud *thump*. "And that's it for the day, children. Good work."

Abby looked up lazily. The trade winds were almost nonexistent today, and the heat made her sleepy. But coming toward them as they sat under the trees was Reese Cutter. The expression on his face made Abby sit up straight. "Luke," she whispered, warning him.

As Reese drew near, Abby realized he looked cool and fresh, dressed in black pants, a white shirt, and a dark green vest—just the opposite of Pa and Uncle Samuel when they came in from their day in the fields.

"Hello, Mrs. Kendall," he said, touching his black moustache. "I thought you might appreciate receiving Mr. Kendall's first paycheck before the store closes for the day."

Ma rose gracefully and took the scrip he handed her. "Why, thank you. That's thoughtful."

He gave a slight bow, then turned his attention on Abby and Luke briefly. "We had visitors last night at the mansion," he said, piercing them with dark eyes. When he withdrew a yellow candle stub from his pocket, Abby heard Luke draw in his breath. Mr. Cutter held it up for all to see. "Anyone care to claim their candle? I found it in my office last night."

Abby felt her stomach turn over. No one said a word as his gaze roamed the group. "But it could well have been the little people—the *menehune*," he concluded, smiling graciously. Then he changed the subject. "What have we here?" he asked. "A portable school?"

"Yes," Ma answered. "I teach my children so they can keep up their lessons."

"What about these others?" Cutter nodded at the Hawaiian children.

"The more the merrier," Ma said lightheartedly.

Reese's eyebrows rose, and his smile dimmed. "How kind of you." He gave a slight bow and took his leave.

Ma turned to Abby excitedly. "Why don't we go shopping right now? If Malama has some rock candy to purchase, we can have a treat."

"But, Ma," Sarah piped up, "Malama says we don't need to buy candy on a sugar plantation when—"

Kini pinched Sarah's arm. "Shhh," he whispered. "Rock candy be good, too."

Sarah rubbed her arm. "Yeah, I forgot."

"Let's go," Ma said. "Everyone deserves a treat for working hard."

They shook out and folded the blanket, then headed for the company store not far away. As they walked, Abby caught Luke's eye. She leaned toward him. "Thank goodness he didn't know it was us!" she whispered fiercely.

Luke grimaced. "I'm sorry I forgot the candle."

"Remember, Luke," Abby teased, "private detectives have to be secretive." When he chuckled, her nerves finally began to relax.

As they entered the cool interior of the store, Ma borrowed one of the baskets stacked by the door and began walking the aisles. The children rushed to the counter where a large glass jar held yellow, red, and green rock candy. Eagerly, they began pointing out the color each one wanted.

Soon Ma arrived back at the counter, her lips pursed. "Malama," she said, "it's a good thing we have our own money, or I couldn't keep my family fed properly with these prices." The basket hung empty on her arm as she recounted the scrip in her hand. "I know Thomas only worked three days, but even with a full week's pay, we would be hard-pressed! What about the other plantation workers?"

Abby held her breath. Would the gracious Hawaiian be offended by Ma's honesty?

Malama shook her head. "Oh, I know, I know. That be the problem we be living with since the Cutter parents died. . . . So many be in debt to Mr. Reese now, they can't leave even though they want to. They can't put aside enough to start somewhere else."

Ma looked shocked. "Well! That explains why he doesn't pay anyone in cash." She turned away, searching for other items.

After helping Ma, Malama asked Abby and the others, "You *keikis* be working hard at school?" When the children chorused "yes," she dipped into the candy jar and gave each child the candy of his or her choice. "No charge," she said with a wink.

As the younger kids wandered off to look at other things, Abby leaned across the counter to Malama. "We've seen the will you talked about. The witness who signed it was Captain Jim Canter."

"How can that be?" Malama exclaimed, her nut-brown eyes surprised. "Mr. and Mrs. Cutter, they did not like that rogue. They would never have him be witness!"

"That's what we think, too," Luke said.

Malama frowned. "That man come to the big house tonight for dinner with Mr. Reese. He always come when he load the sugar on his ship."

Abby nodded. "His ship is the *Beauty*?"

"Yes, that be the name."

"We're familiar with it," Abby said, glancing

86

sideways at Luke. But before she could say more, Ma arrived with a somber look on her face.

"I guess this will be it for now, Malama." She handed over just a few items and all of the scrip Reese had given her.

As they exited the little store, Malama walked them out. "*Aloha*," she said cheerfully. "You *keikis* keep up your schoolwork and I give you more treats." But she bent down and gave Kini an extra hug. His dark brown eyes gazed up into hers as she spoke gently to him. "You come to my hut tonight, Kini? I need help. Hoku and I have too much *poi* to eat. It go bad soon if I not get some help."

Kini's grin flashed quickly. "I come, Malama. I be glad to help."

"Good," she said fondly. "I look for you at dinnertime."

Ma smiled at Malama. Abby knew Ma understood how lonely Kini was for his own family, and Malama and Hoku seemed to have taken Kini into their hearts.

Abby walked slowly on purpose, letting everyone go on ahead. But in a minute, Luke turned and waited for her. "What are you doing, writing a poem?"

She smiled at his teasing. "No, I'm thinking about tonight."

Luke looked confused. "What about it?"

"It might be our only chance to investigate, you goose!"

Luke raked a hand through his straight hair. "Investigate what? After last night, I'm surprised you'd think of doing it again."

"We haven't got any choice. We have to go check out Cap'n Jim's cabin, of course. While he's here eating dinner tonight, we'll have to hurry to Nawiliwili Harbor and search the *Beauty*."

Luke took a deep breath. "I don't think that's wise. If we get caught by Cap'n Jim, he's liable to sell us as slaves in China."

"The ship might still be at the dock."

Luke pierced her with green eyes. "Aren't you listening to me? It's too dangerous, Abby. He hasn't got a nice bone in his body."

"Luke, we haven't got a choice! The *Beauty* will be leaving soon, and this could be our only chance to solve the mystery of the will. And we *know* Cap'n Jim is somehow connected to Duncan's father's disappearance. Don't you want to help Duncan?"

Luke cracked his knuckles nervously. "All right, I'll go alone. That way, if I get caught, at least you can send in the cavalry to rescue me."

"No deal," Abby said, spreading her feet like she was getting ready to throw a punch. "We're a team. Duncan's part of it, too. We have to know if there's anything on board that links Cap'n Jim to Duncan's father. And with two of us working, the search will go twice as fast."

Luke exhaled. He finally nodded slowly as if digesting the idea. "You're right. We can't wait for

Duncan—the *Beauty* could sail before he gets back."

"We'll never get another chance like this to help Duncan," Abby reminded him. But even as she said it, she thought about the near miss they'd had at Reese Cutter's mansion. Should they risk it again? Because if Cap'n Jim caught them, Luke was right.

The consequences were bound to be a disaster.

Chapter Nine

As soon as dinner was done, Abby and Luke volunteered to do the dishes so they could talk.

"We'll have to ask Lani if we can borrow a horse from the stables," Abby said. "It's the only way we can get to the harbor and back quickly."

Now that she'd convinced Luke to investigate the *Beauty*, he was eager to get it done. The thought of sneaking on board a ship full of scalawags didn't sound appealing to either of them. But one thing Luke had always admired about Abby was her spunk.

"All right, let's go." He'd heard Abby tell her ma that they were going to visit Lani. As they left camp, he noted that Sandy was curled up in Sarah's lap. Hopefully, the pup would stay asleep and not come looking for him until the two of them returned.

They walked the short way to Lani's hut, and Abby poked her head in the open door. "Lani, you home?"

"Come in," Lani said, her blue eyes lighting up. "I was just going to look for you two."

"You were?" Luke asked, puzzled. "You need help with something?"

"Exactly. Reese told me to take tomorrow off. He could see how tired I am from Mother's funeral, the feast, and all the hard work lately, and I have a promise to keep. I'd love it if you would come with me tomorrow to a special place. Mother called it her 'hiding place.' It was where she went to remember my father. They had spent time together there years ago."

Abby's face shone with anticipation. "We'd love to! Where is it?"

"It's far. We'll have to ride horses, bring a lunch, and travel north past a fern grotto."

Luke grinned. "Sounds like an adventure. What do we do when we get there?"

"Actually, I promised Mother I'd collect some of her things from her getaway and bring them back here. But I thought you two might enjoy a swim at the waterfall. We'll also pass some of the stone aqueducts. You know, the ones that the *menehune* are supposed to have made so long ago."

"Count us in," Luke said happily, thinking that exploring a new area sounded fun.

"Actually, Lani," Abby began, "we came to see how you're doing but also to ask your permission to borrow a horse for an evening ride."

Lani gazed at them for a few seconds, her sky blue eyes warm and curious. Luke's pulse sped up. If Lani said no, they'd be out of luck.

"Of course. If you can find the groom, ask him to saddle Sea Breeze. She's gentle."

Luke felt a rush of relief. "Thanks, Lani. We won't be out too long."

Luke and Abby hurried to the stables, which were down the road from the mansion. When they didn't see anyone around, they decided to find Sea Breeze by themselves. Each went down opposite rows of stalls, reading the horses' nameplates. "Here she is," Luke called out to Abby, who had headed off in the other direction of the long cool stable.

As he opened Sea Breeze's stall, the palomino mare whinnied a greeting and tossed her ivory mane.

"Oh, Luke, she's beautiful," Abby said, arriving at the stall.

Luke rubbed the palomino's golden nose as he slipped on her bridle. "Friendly, too," he said.

They mounted her bareback, which would be easier with two of them riding.

As they trotted by the big house, Abby spoke up. "Look, there are two horses tied up out front. That must mean Cap'n Jim and one of his mates are here right now."

"Let's hope so," Luke said.

There was still sunlight left. It would be another half hour before darkness fell, but Luke spurred the mare into a canter down the dirt road. They had much to do before the captain returned to his ship.

As they neared Nawiliwili Harbor, Luke slowed Sea Breeze to a walk. "We've got to find a place to stash the horse," he said.

"How about that stand of hibiscus over there?" Abby suggested.

Sure enough, the shrubs were tall and thick, with plenty of greenery all about for the mare to browse. "She'll love it," he said as he directed her to it. They quickly dismounted and tied her to a kiawe tree that stood in the middle of the stand.

It didn't take long to spot the *Beauty*. As they watched 100 feet from the harbor, they could see that the ship was moored to a dock with her gangplank down, just as they'd hoped. For a few minutes, they searched for activity on board, but no sailors appeared to be around. "The crew might be ashore," he said, "but there's bound to be someone on watch. Let's head over and scout it out. Act casual."

Silently they crept down the wooden dock. When they drew even with the black ship, Luke ducked behind some barrels on the jetty. Abby followed.

"There are two sailors drinking in the stern," he whispered.

"Yeah, and they're facing out to sea. Looks like they're the only ones here, too," Abby answered.

"Then let's go." He stood up and ran lightly up the gangplank, crouching low when he came on board. Abby joined him seconds later.

"My heart's thundering," she said.

He grinned. "Just like old times. Remember our escape from Jackal's ship?"

Together they made their way to the hatch and climbed below the deck, following the hallway to the last cabin in the stern. Below the deck, the ship was just as decrepit and dirty as above. Luke whispered, "They're directly above us. We've got to be really quiet now."

Abby nodded, then pushed the latch on the captain's cabin door. As she entered, she quickly covered her nose. "It stinks in here!"

Luke grimaced at the smell. "It's the stench of old whiskey breath and stale food." As they glanced around the dimly lit cabin, they were shocked to see piles of clothes, dirty dishes, and maps littering the bunk, center table, and desk. Even the window seat was piled high with clutter, and the floor was covered with empty whiskey bottles that rolled occasionally with the ship's movement. In the darkness, Abby moved forward, then yelped quietly.

"Are you all right?" Luke whispered.

"Yes," Abby muttered. "I just stepped on something and twisted my ankle."

Luke watched her bend down and retrieve an old

cork that had once been a stopper to one of the many bottles now on the floor.

"This is the culprit," she whispered, stuffing it into her skirt pocket.

Luke lit the lantern on the table, turning it down to a bare-minimum flame.

Without any more conversation, they set to work—both beginning their search for clues.

The search was made more difficult by the mess. They had to move piles to get to drawers and cupboards. Then they had to replace piles. Finally after half an hour, Luke lifted the window seat. Under a blanket he discovered a small tin chest, which he quickly brought to the lantern on the table.

Abby hurried over. "What is it?"

"A sea chest, but look at the initials on the top," he said. They stared silently at the letters clearly engraved before them.

"I. A. M.," Abby said softly. "The same letters as Duncan's father's initials. Ian Argyle MacIndou. Could it be his chest?"

"If it is," Luke said slowly, "then it's the proof we need that Cap'n Jim was somehow involved in Ian's disappearance. Otherwise, why would Cap'n Jim have his chest? And if it's not Duncan's father's chest, whose else could it be? Those are unusual initials."

"Cap'n Jim murdered him," Abby said angrily. "I'm sure of it."

"Let's look inside."

But that was easier said than done. It was locked, and there was no key in sight. Luke went to the desk and searched for something to pry it open. He quickly returned with a silver letter opener.

After 10 agonizing minutes, the lock finally gave. Abby wrung her hands nervously. "Luke, we have to hurry. This is taking too long. I'm beginning to get a bad feeling. . . ."

"I know," he said, nervous himself. "But we're not done."

They rifled through a stack of papers, holding up each one to the light. Just as Luke was about to give up hope of finding any more evidence, Abby gasped.

"This one's addressed to Mr. George Cutter. Reese Cutter's father."

Luke moved closer as Abby turned the page over to glimpse the signature.

"Oh, my goodness! The letter's signed by Ian MacIndou! Luke, this *is* his sea chest!"

"What's he doing writing to Mr. Cutter?" Luke queried.

Abby scanned the contents. "The letter asks Mr. Cutter to help Kalele, Ian's new wife. Listen—," Abby whispered. She found the place on the page and began reading.

"'If anything should happen to me and I don't return, please help Kalele. She has risked everything to marry me. By doing so, she has angered a power-ful family on Kauai, whose son she was supposed to have wed. I have sent her my belongings and a similar letter, telling her that she can find refuge and work with you.'"

Abby and Luke stared at each other in awe. "This letter is proof that Cap'n Jim was somehow involved in Ian MacIndou's life. After all, he has his sea chest. But why is this letter here? Why didn't it get to Mr. Cutter?"

"Because James Canter is a bilge rat," Luke whispered angrily. "Maybe he was asked to deliver the letter to Mr. Cutter—and he didn't." He was quiet for a moment. "But what about the other letter MacIndou mentions? The one that he sent to Kalele? Do you think that letter made it to her?"

"Well, no one on the plantation ever heard of Kalele," Abby said in a puzzled tone. "Duncan asked all around before he left. . . . You don't think something happened to Kalele, too, do you?" she asked, horror in her eyes.

Luke swallowed hard. "I don't know. Let's keep looking to see if there's anything else."

Minutes passed as they searched through the rest of the papers. Occasionally they heard noises overhead from the sailors on watch. Most of what they found was related to shipping contracts. One was even a contract from Reese Cutter for Cpn. Jim Canter to ship cane and molasses to Honolulu regularly. Luke scanned it before passing it over to Abby. One sentence stuck out, so he read Reese Cutter's words to Abby.

"'Now that I am sole heir and owner of this grand estate, you shall deal directly with me.'" The contract was dated six years ago.

Abby made no comment but went on searching. "We've got to get out of here soon," she whispered as she picked up the last sheet of paper in the bottom of the trunk.

Just then a terrifying sound rang out. "Ho, Captain! Welcome aboard. How was dinner?" Heavy boots pounded down the dock, and panic surged through Luke and Abby as the deep voices came closer with every step.

She and Luke glanced at the final paper she now clutched: *Last Will and Testament.*

"Come on," Luke urged. "There's no time to read it now." He leaned over and blew out the lantern, listening to the footfalls coming. *How are we going to escape with our path blocked?*

Chapter Ten

Quickly they threw all the papers into the chest except for the letter from Duncan's father and the will Abby had just found. As Luke rushed to place the sea chest back in the window seat, he accidently kicked an empty bottle. It went skittering across the wood floor, and they froze in their tracks.

Abby and Luke cocked their heads. Had they been discovered?

But it seemed the loud voices and footfalls had covered the noise. They could hear the sailors coming closer by the second!

Luke rushed to the window above the window seat, but the latch was jammed. He strained with all his might—grunting with effort. "It's no use," he said desperately.

Abby pointed at a porthole that looked away from the dock and out into the bay. "This way, Luke!" The latch flipped up, and she pushed the window open easily.

Luke eyed the porthole, realizing it was the only way. Darkness had fallen, so most likely they wouldn't be seen. And the voices and sounds of boots were almost upon them! "This is the only option," he whispered fiercely, as he dragged a chair for Abby to climb up.

"The papers will get wet, Luke!"

In a panic, Luke's eyes roamed the room for something, anything, in which to store their clues.

"The ink will run, and it's all we have as proof for Duncan," she said.

He bent down to retrieve an old whiskey bottle and handed it to her. Rolling the papers together, she shoved them in and stopped the bottle with the cork from her skirt pocket.

"Now it's over the side with you," Luke urged as he took the bottle from her.

It was a tight squeeze, but Abby climbed on the seat and jammed her legs through the porthole first. Perching on it momentarily, she allowed her body to slide ungracefully out. She dropped into the salty bay waters below with a splash, then tread water while waiting for Luke.

Suddenly the whiskey bottle came sailing out the porthole, narrowly missing her head. She grabbed it and began trying to stuff it into her soggy skirt pocket.

She tried not to think about large fish swimming below her feet as she watched for Luke. First his feet slid out the window, followed by his long legs and torso. But then he appeared stuck. Were his shoulders too wide for the opening? *Dear Lord*, she prayed, *help us!*

Luke could hear the captain's voice talking loudly now. His shoulders were stuck, but a surge of adrenaline shot through him and he pushed hard. He could hear his shirt rip, and as his shoulders finally squeezed through the tight spot, he skinned himself. But he fell out of the porthole and toward the black water just as the door burst open.

A few seconds later, Luke surfaced and kicked toward Abby. Both saw a lantern go on in the captain's cabin. Desperate to escape, they swam toward the dock in the dark warm sea and found a place to climb out.

They emerged dripping and ran up the slope to the hibiscus grove. Sea Breeze whinnied a greeting, and Luke gave Abby a leg up, then jumped up behind her. As he urged the horse into a canter, he felt his muscles begin to relax. "You've got the bottle?"

"What bottle?"

Luke almost fell off the horse. "The bottle with the letters in it!"

Abby turned halfway around, and he could see her mischievous smile. "You deserved that for almost knocking me out when you dropped it."

Too relieved to be angry, Luke chuckled. "Sure glad we don't have to go back."

The balmy night breeze, scented with wild *pikake,* quickly dried their clothes as they cantered home.

As soon as they returned Sea Breeze to her stall, Abby raced to her hut. The bottle was still hidden in her pocket. They had made it home safely, but a light was on in her hut.

As she entered, Pa glanced up. "We were just coming to look for you," Pa said. He had one boot on, the other in his hand.

"Sorry I'm late, Pa. We took a night ride, and my hair's come undone." She quickly went to her bed, where Sarah lay almost asleep.

"Say your prayers, honey," Ma urged as Pa blew out the light. "And don't make us worry again. I know it's safe here, but you still need to be home by dark from now on."

"Yes, Ma." Abby changed into her nightdress. She lay down softly and listened to the sounds of the evening. Crickets and the song of some unknown bird soothed her tense nerves. *Thank You for the help, Lord. Please send Duncan back soon to help us unravel this mystery.*

Just before she fell asleep, she slipped the bottle into her satchel, under her clothes. Tomorrow would be soon enough to read the mysterious will.

"Luke!" Abby jumped up and down in excitement. Ma was frying eggs over the campfire for breakfast, the puppy was barking ferociously at a gecko, and Sarah and Kini were chasing each other around a log.

"It's awfully early to be so worked up, Abby." Curiosity lit up Luke's eyes. "What is it?"

She pulled him into the hut, which was empty at the moment, and took the will out of her satchel. "Malama was more right than she knew, Luke—about the Cutter parents wanting to give something back to the workers. The first will we saw wasn't the original will. Here's the *real* will they wrote! And we found it!"

Luke's shocked eyes veered to the paper. "Jehoshaphat!" He sat down and devoured the will with an eager gaze.

"Can you believe it?" Abby asked. "It's even better than Malama could have hoped."

"Why on earth was this in Cap'n Jim's cabin?"

"That's part of the mystery I hope Duncan can help us unravel," Abby said brightly as she took the will and stuffed it back under her clothes. "Let's not mention it to anyone until we talk to Duncan, all right? He should be back any day now."

Chapter Eleven

No sooner had Abby finished her chores than Lani rode up on a roan mare, with Sea Breeze, the golden palomino, reined in at her side. "Are you ready?" she called out brightly.

Abby grinned at the beautiful picture she made. Lani's long chestnut hair was tied back in a ponytail, and her white shirt was tucked crisply into her full green skirt. The leather thongs of her Roman-style sandals were tied around her slim ankles.

"There's a lot to see," Lani urged, "and I've packed a lunch."

Luke came bounding over from his hut. "Did I hear you say 'lunch'?" His cheek dimpled as he grinned and rubbed his belly.

Lani laughed and tossed him the reins to Sea Breeze, who shook her head and pawed the ground as if she, too, was eager to be off while the morning was still cool and fresh.

"Bye, Ma!" Abby hollered as she mounted Sea

Breeze with Luke's help and placed her satchel in front of her. "We'll be back by nightfall."

Charlotte looked up from the dishes she was drying and smiled. "Have fun," she said, waving the towel at them.

After Luke mounted the horse to sit behind Abby, they rode off down the lane leading back to the main road.

Abby asked Luke, "Who's watching Sandy?"

"Kini," Luke answered from behind her. "Who's watching Sarah?"

"Ma." Abby relaxed at the thought of a day away from all responsibilities, then turned her attention to the scenery as they journeyed northward together.

The farther they traveled, the more varied the view became. From rocky slopes of grassland to ravines with lush vegetation, their eyes feasted on the sights. Abby breathed deeply. She reached into her bag and withdrew her journal and pencil. The fragrance of Hawaiian ginger and *pikake* scented the air. And the lovely blooms of red hibiscus, yellow passionflowers, and white orchids grew among glimmering green leaves.

Passing under a plumeria tree, Luke plucked a blossom and handed it to Abby. She turned to smile into his green eyes as she tucked the flower into her braid.

She noticed Luke's freckles were disappearing under a dark tan, which had come from weeks at sea. Other things about Luke had changed, too, she reflected. The pain of losing his parents, which she'd seen in him for years, was being replaced by joy. *It's as if things have finally been set right in his world,* she thought. *And they have!*

Opening to a fresh page in her journal, Abby rode along, struggling to capture an idea in a poem. She wrote, erased, then wrote some more. When it was done, she read it aloud to Lani and Luke.

> *"The world is like a garden,*
>   *where sweet blossoms abound,*
> *and high above, the windblown trees*
>   *make a lovely sound.*
> *More lovely still is sunlight,*
>   *which banishes all gloom,*
> *like God, who sets all things right,*
>   *so that His children bloom."*

"Abby, that's great!" Luke said. It was the first time he'd ever praised her poems instead of making fun of them, and she found herself blushing. But secretly she was happy, for the words of the poem were exactly what she'd wanted to say—even though no words could capture the feelings of joy she had regarding Luke, who had finally made peace with God. In spite of losing his parents, having to deal with his mean aunt, and mourning the loss of his dog, Sparks, the Lord had filled him with a newfound peace.

Every morning Luke listened carefully as Ma read from her Bible. And later in the day he'd often bring up the passage to Abby, as if he'd been chewing it over.

Through his enthusiasm, Abby was seeing the Word of God in a new light. His excitement was contagious. Abby closed her journal contentedly and slipped it into her bag.

A few minutes later, they passed a gigantic stone fishpond, still in use by the locals. "Tradition says this was built," Lani said, "by the *menehune*. It's been here a long time, perhaps 1,000 years."

Luke whistled. "Talk about quality work that lasts! What are these *menehune* supposed to look like, Lani?"

"Well," she said laughing, "I've heard stories that they are little fellows. They'd come no higher than your waist, Luke. With their big eyes, they have great eyesight. And perhaps because they lift so many stones, they are said to have red faces."

"What do people say about why they left and where they went?" Abby asked.

"Some believe they left Kauai when the Tahitians arrived and went back to the lost continent of Mu. Others say they are living in hidden valleys on this island, in secret places where no one ever ventures. That's why Hawaiians say that if there's mischief afoot, it's the *menehune*."

For a while the well-worn path led beside the sea, where the refreshing breeze kept them cool. Then they headed inland along Wailua River toward a fern grotto, a special place Lani wanted Abby and Luke to experience. When they arrived, they dismounted and walked to a glen forested with huge ferns, some as tall as Abby. Lani led them deeper through the moist tropics, into a cave mouth that soared 40 feet overhead.

Water droplets rained down, and rivulets trickled over the cave's side, then out to the nearby river. Dark green ferns dotted the walls, which formed a natural amphitheater. "Many come here to be married," Lani explained. "Isn't it enchanting?"

Even Luke marveled at the natural beauty of the flowers and glistening rock walls. "It sure is pretty," he said softly, but his statement echoed loudly in the cave.

When Abby giggled, her laughter bounced off rocks and ricocheted back to her. Soon they were yodelling like the Swiss.

"If you think this is fun," Lani said, "wait 'til you see the next stop."

"Hope there's a papaya tree close by," Luke commented. "I'm hungry." When his stomach growled, the cave magnified it to a rumble, and they all chuckled.

Twenty minutes later, they arrived at a fork in the river. Lani led them to an overgrown path that led down, down, down through dark shade trees. "Few know about this trail," she said, "but it leads to my favorite swimming hole."

As she finished speaking, the horses broke into sunlight. There before them was a waterfall that cascaded 20 feet through the air into a beautiful green pool of freshwater. "Oh, Lani," Abby said with a sigh, "it's delicious."

"Almost as welcome as food would be right now," Luke added.

Lani grinned as she tossed him her saddlebag. "I've packed enough food for a growing boy," she said as she dismounted. "The horses can graze, while we do the same."

She untied a blanket roll from her saddle and spread it on the natural lawn, and Luke hurried over to empty the saddlebag. Inside were wonderful treats: ham sandwiches, ripe mangoes, fresh-baked pineapple cookies, macadamia-nut candy, and a jug of tea.

Half an hour later, after three sandwiches and eight cookies, Luke lay fast asleep. But Abby and Lani were deep in conversation.

"How did you learn about this wonderful place?" Abby asked.

"Mother took me to her secret hiding place every year. We are very close to it now. When she and my father were married, they stayed there for a while before he had to leave. So it held special memories for her. She kept a few of his things there. At least once a year my mother and I would travel here to repair the grass hut. And on the way, we'd always stop at this pool to play."

Lani pointed to the waterfall 20 feet above the deep, green pool. "See the river cascading down? Many years ago Mother took me down the waterfall."

Abby looked curious. "You jumped?"

"No, the rocks form a natural slide. It's smooth and slick. Mother and I flew down the slide and sailed through the air, then splashed into the cool water. I loved it."

I hate heights, Abby thought nervously. But she was so hot, and the idea was so inviting. "Lani, let's do it!" she urged. "How do you get up there?"

"I'm afraid you have to retrace your steps a long way . . . or you could climb the rock wall. But it looks wet and slippery."

Abby was already taking off her sandals. "I'm willing if you are."

Lani grinned and untied her sandals. Together they hiked around the pool until they got to the rock face. Then each tied her long skirt into a knot by her knees and began the climb, one rock at a time. Abby soon learned that the higher she went, the slipperier the stones became with water and moss. As Abby's legs began to weaken with the effort of the climb, she began to sweat with fear.

But Lani waited patiently for her, and Abby

followed in her footsteps. In 15 minutes they had scaled the wall and were standing near the cliff edge where the water cascaded. As they swam out in the stream from which the water plunged over the edge, Abby hollered to wake up Luke. She didn't want him to miss this!

The water's movement pulled Abby and Lani toward the edge of the cliff, but it wasn't strong enough to whisk them over the side. So they had time to arrange themselves on the rocks that shot out over the pool. They pushed off against the slippery rocks, and Abby screamed again. As they plunged down the rock slide, she could see Luke sitting up and looking wildly around for them.

Abby would never forget the amazement on his face as she, with Lani sitting behind her, went slipping down the slide and flying through the air. They sailed out, then punctured the pool's surface with a tremendous splash.

When they surfaced, Luke stood gaping at the pool's edge. "Jehoshaphat! That was great!"

Abby and Lani scrambled out and took Luke with them on their next climb. For over an hour they screamed and splashed and chased one another over the waterfall. Abby's legs quivered with exhaustion by the time they lay down to rest on the blanket. But in the heat their clothes were soon dry, so Lani persuaded them to remount. "We're almost there," she promised. "We're almost at my mother's hiding place."

Chapter Twelve

Naomi's special place wasn't far from the waterfall. Surrounded by ohi'a trees aflame with delicate red *lehua* blossoms, the hut stood hidden and silent.

They tied their mounts to bushes and pushed open the sagging door. It would have been dim inside, but part of the thatched roof had fallen in, letting in sunlight. On their right stood a crude rope-mattress bedstead. Next to it was a barrel covered with a plank of wood for a tabletop. Two candles sat on top of it. Packing crates were piled against one wall, forming a simple bookshelf on which a few objects sat. The floor was earth-packed.

Lani grew quiet as she entered with Luke and Abby at her side. Abby suspected the hut brought back memories, making Lani realize that she'd never come here again with her dear mother.

"Shall I fix the roof?" Luke asked.

Lani looked up into the trees that towered above the hut. "No, it's not important now. This is probably the last time I will come. Mother wanted me to retrieve the last few things here and say good-bye to her special place."

"Then I think I'll take a look around the forest," Luke said as he walked back out.

Lani invited Abby to sit on the bed while she went through her mother's belongings. She crossed the small room to the barrel and set aside the wooden board that covered it.

As she removed a folded quilt and other items, she spoke from her heart. "Mother relied on God when she learned my father had been killed. . . . She told me all about him, but I wish I could have known him."

She withdrew another item and handed it to Abby. "My father made this for Mother." It was a delicately carved bird. "A honeycreeper," Lani said. "See the long hooked beak that draws nectar from the flower?"

It was beautiful. But as Abby turned the silky-smooth carving in her hands, her mind began to race. *I've never seen such intricate woodwork before . . . except for . . . of course!* She remembered suddenly. *The dolphin carved by Duncan's father.*

She was about to comment, but Lani was busy, glancing through a slim stack of papers she'd found in the bottom of the barrel. She read silently for a few minutes, then gazed up at Abby. "I've never seen these papers before." She frowned, then went on. "After Father died, Mother came to work for the Cutters. She took another name, Naomi, because that's the woman from the Bible who lost her husband, too."

Abby gasped. "Another *name?*" she asked. "Then what was your mother's real name?"

Lani looked up from the papers absentmindedly. "Oh, her other name? My father loved her real name, she said, because it means 'to lean on for support.' Isn't that lovely? He said she was his support. Her real Hawaiian name was Kalele."

Abby's mouth dropped open. At the same moment Luke walked through the open door, and their eyes locked. Turning to Lani, he asked, "Did you *just* say Kalele?"

"Yes, why? Does it mean something to you?" Lani asked calmly, her eyes skimming the papers.

Abby and Luke stared at one another silently. *Should we tell her what we know?* Abby wondered. *Or should we wait until Duncan returns—so he can tell her that we've been searching for Kalele?*

Lani seemed engrossed as she said, "I've never seen these before. But on her deathbed Mother said there was information here that I should know. But I'm confused by this page." She held up a letter, which Abby scooted over to share with her.

Abby's heart began to pound like a gourd drum. It was the missing letter! The one Ian MacIndou had written to Kalele before his death, urging her to seek out the Cutters if he did not return!

Lani turned the page over, read the signature at the bottom, then looked up, confused. "I don't understand. Mother always called Father 'Kamana.' That word means 'carpenter.' And I knew my father worked with wood. But this letter is signed 'Ian MacIndou.'" Lani frowned, then tensed as if someone had struck her. "Your friend, Duncan, whom I met over dinner that night—isn't MacIndou his last name, too? Do you think there could be some connection between Duncan and my father?"

"Yes," Abby said, her heart sure of the answer.

Luke spoke up solemnly. "If your father is Ian MacIndou, that makes Duncan your half brother."

Lani sat back, stunned. She swallowed hard and then reread the letter. "Yes, this is from my father. But Mother never told me his English name. She said she couldn't tell me, that she had to protect me. But she never told me whom she was protecting me from."

"I think I know," Abby said quietly. "According to Ian's diary that we found, your mother was supposed to marry a powerful chief on Kauai. But she fell in love with Ian and married him instead. Maybe this chief got angry and was looking for her."

"And that's why she took another name— Naomi," Luke finished.

"That has to be it," Lani said. "But I can hardly believe I've found the answer after all these years. After Mother's death." She pressed one hand to her temple. "This is a lot to take in." She sat silently a moment longer, then turned to Abby. "Mother and

I were alone for a long time. When she died, I felt even more alone in the world. But if I have a brother, I won't be alone. And I'm eager to get to know him!"

Abby threw her arms around Lani, glad the news made her happy. "Well, Duncan should be coming back anytime now."

"Then let's go," Lani said. Her whole face lit up. "I must speak with him! And right away!"

Chapter Thirteen

The three travelers arrived back at the plantation at the end of the day. The sun was casting golden threads of light across the land as they passed by Cutter Grove Cemetery on their way back to the stables.

Through the open gate of the white picket fence, Abby saw two *kanakas* wrestling a gray headstone into place over Naomi's grave. "Look, Lani," she said, pointing. "Your mother's marker has arrived."

The three got off their horses, and Lani struck up a conversation with the two Hawaiians, who were fellow workers on the plantation. "It sat in front of the mansion all day," one of the laborers told her, "but we finally had time to bring it here."

"*Mahalo,*" Lani said softly as they left.

Abby and Luke stood nearby, reading the words of the headstone along with Lani. "In Loving Memory of Naomi Kamana, once called Kalele, Whose God Was Her Refuge and Strength."

Plumeria blossoms were carved in a wreath around the words.

"It's beautiful," Abby said.

Lani only nodded and wiped a tear.

They dropped the horses off at the stables, then quietly headed toward their huts. But in the failing light, they could see Reese Cutter striding toward them.

As he drew near, he smoothed his jet-black moustache and eyed Lani speculatively. He got right to the point without a hello. "Jim Canter was here today. For some reason he was interested in your mother's gravestone when he saw it. He asked about your mother's circumstances . . . said he once knew a Kalele. I couldn't tell him anything except that he could come back tomorrow to talk to you." He rubbed his jaw. "Isn't Kalele the name Duncan MacIndou was asking about, too?"

Lani pursed her lips. "I didn't hear him mention that name," she answered.

Reese nodded slowly, his face calm. "Did you have a good day off, Lani? You look relaxed."

She rubbed her arms, as if suddenly chilled. "Yes," she said. "Thanks for the time away." Then she headed toward her hut.

Abby saw emotion flicker briefly across Reese's face as he turned to go back to the big house. Was he hurt that Lani had snubbed him?

"We best go, too," Luke mumbled, and Abby followed him to the fire pit in front of her grass hut.

"We need to talk," he said, pointing to the fallen koa log in front of the low fire. Abby sat down, but Luke paced back and forth before he stopped and faced her.

"I don't trust Cutter, Abby. He's full of oily words, but I think they're for his own gain." Luke's agitation showed as he began pacing again. "And if he knew about the real will, then he's cheating his own workers! That's big. Your ma read that Bible verse the other day about knowing a tree by its fruit. It's the same with people. Cutter's got rotten fruit."

Abby stood up and faced him. "But, Luke, I've seen both good and bad fruit in Reese. First he gives Uncle Samuel and Pa jobs, he gives us places to stay, and then a birthday party for Sarah. But he's also the one who closed the school. How can we tell what kind of person he really is?"

Luke shook his head. "I don't know all the answers. I'm just warning you to watch your back around him."

Abby exhaled in frustration. "I want to believe the best, but I admit—I'm confused." She thought of Reese's face when Lani walked away from him. *Was it anger or hurt that I saw there?*

"Right now," Luke said, "the Almighty's the only One who knows. So let's pray about it." He gave her a half smile, then headed toward his hut.

Abby listened to the sound of his footsteps moving away through the darkness. *Why is life so complicated?* she wondered as she entered her family's hut. Ma and Pa were talking quietly by candlelight, and Sarah was playing with her new doll on their straw-stuffed mattress. Soon Abby was ready for bed, too, but after the light went out, she had a hard time falling asleep.

And when she finally did, bad dreams haunted her.

Abby woke in pitch black, her heart pounding. She could feel Sarah's leg pressed against hers. The soft sighs of the wind weaving through the grass walls comforted her as she realized a bad dream had jarred her awake.

She couldn't remember details of the nightmare, only that someone had been chasing her and she couldn't outrun him. He was gaining on her. She could hear him crashing through the thicket after her. The dream haunted her for a few moments until Pa's light snores erupted from the other side of the hut. Abby turned over, happy to be safe in bed. *Thank goodness it was only a dream.*

Then why did she still hear a faint crashing? The sound made her sit up.

For a moment, all was quiet. Then she heard it again. A muffled sound, like someone scuffling nearby. Maybe an animal was into Ma's store of food. Pa snored on. Apparently, it wasn't loud enough to wake the others.

Rising quietly, Abby slipped off her nightdress and pulled on her nearby skirt and blouse. She hastily tied her sandals and hurried out the door to shoo away the midnight visitor. But a few steps from her door, Abby could see nothing amiss around their campfire. The continued noises drew her forward, and she noticed a faint light emanating from Lani's hut. Muffled voices were coming from it as well!

She hurried toward the grass dwelling, anxiety curling in her stomach. As she reached the hut, another muffled crash sounded, and Abby's concern propelled her forward. She threw open the door and gasped at the sight that met her.

Lani's clothes were strewn everywhere, and the bed mattress lay ripped open on the floor. But worse, Lani's arms were gripped from behind by Cap'n Jim! The beautiful Hawaiian woman looked small and thin beside his hulking frame, and her face showed a desperate fear when she turned toward Abby.

"Run!" Lani said, but Abby's first thought was to spring into action to help.

Just as she opened her mouth to scream and rush forward, a rough hand clamped over Abby's lips. Someone strong and tall secured her arms in a painful grip. Cap'n Jim pierced Abby with a smug look. "Keep quiet or the woman gets hurt," he ordered, touching the pistol in his belt. "You understand?"

Abby's eyes veered to Lani's face. She nodded for Abby to obey, and Abby dipped her head once in surrender.

Cap'n Jim removed the pistol from his belt and waved it at Lani. "Move out quiet-like, or someone will pay the price."

Abby and Lani, who was still in her long night-dress, were pushed through the door by Cap'n Jim and his cohort, a silent, muscular man. They were herded into a nearby grove of trees. The wind blew and the branches swayed, covering the sound of their footsteps as they entered a little clearing a distance from the huts. Abby turned and faced their abductors, wishing Pa would wake and come to their rescue!

She wanted to scream—*Oh, why didn't I do it earlier?*—but Cap'n Jim trained his gun on her or Lani continuously.

Once they were hidden among the trees, Cap'n Jim glared at them. "Where's the gold?" His voice was hard-edged. "I know yer pa had it, so he musta left it fer yer mother. Only I couldn't find Kalele all these years. Not until today. Now that I seen the headstone, I know she musta left the gold to ya."

Lani sat down on a fallen log, her long hair blowing across her face. "I don't know anything about any gold . . . please, let Abby go. She's not part of this."

Cap'n Jim laughed wickedly, and Abby shuddered. The glazed look in his eyes made her think of a rabid wolf. He was beyond reasoning.

When he came over and raised a hand to strike Lani, she cowered. "It's in my shack," she said. "Send Abby to get it."

"It's not there. We been through it all. Even Reese has been through yer pitiful little belongin's. So if ya lie to me again, I'll do worse than hit ya."

Abby couldn't believe her ears. Could it be true? Could Reese, who seemed to love Lani, be in cahoots with Cap'n Jim?

"Listen," Lani said desperately, "why would I work so hard at my job if I had gold? You're crazy to think I have gold!"

Cap'n Jim stepped closer. "Yer mother left it to ya as an inheritance. But yer right, I am crazy!" He laughed like a madman. "To prove it to ya, I'll just shoot this little snippet. Then ya might think about handin' it over."

Lani's mouth twisted in fear. "No! No, I'll take you to the place . . . where it's hidden. But we'll need horses."

Cap'n Jim began to smile, greed evident in his eyes. "Now ye're talkin'. See, Dutch, I told ya we'd get it outta her."

They hurried Abby and Lani to the stables. When a light went on in the stableman's room, Dutch waited outside his door, whacked him soundly with the pistol butt, and tied him up while Cap'n Jim chose which horses to steal.

Abby's stomach was in a cold knot as they began their dangerous journey in the middle of the night. She was sure Lani planned to lead the men to the shack.

But what will happen, Abby wondered, *when we get there and these gutter rats don't find the gold they crave?*

She decided not to think that far ahead. But she began to pray.

Chapter Fourteen

The first glimmers of a rosy dawn showed through the clouds when Luke emerged, yawning, from his hut. Kini and the puppy were still fast asleep, as was Uncle Samuel.

Wandering over to the communal water pump, Luke grinned when he saw a man shaving soapsuds from his cheeks and chin. Duncan was back!

As Duncan swiped at his chin with the straight-edge razor, Luke sneaked up on him and clapped him on the back when he paused. Duncan twirled quickly. "Ye almost made me cut me throat, lad!" He tossed the blade into a little cup and grabbed a towel to dry off his face. "Why are ye up so early?"

Luke grinned. "Glad you're back, Duncan, because I've got great news. But maybe I should wait 'til you finish with your hair and nails and moustache." Everyone knew Duncan was fastidious about cleanliness, but only Luke got away with teasing him.

"I'd like to see ye try," Duncan said as he lunged

at Luke, grabbing his head under his arm in a tight hold. "Do ye give?"

Luke squirmed for a moment, then went lax. "Aye," he said like a Scotsman.

When Luke straightened, he grinned. "Duncan, you won't believe what we've discovered! We found your father's wife, Kalele."

Duncan's mouth popped open. Before he could form a word, however, Luke pressed on.

"And we've also found your half sister."

Duncan pressed fingers to his temple. "Me half sister? Do ye mean to tell me, me da had another child, a daughter with Kalele?"

"Yep, and she's a pretty one, too. But you already know that. It's Lani."

"Whoa, back up, lad. Tell me how you know this to be trrrue." The Scotsman sat down heavily on a stump, while Luke launched into the story of their recent adventures.

"While you were away, Abby and I discovered that Reese Cutter was somehow tied up with Captain Jim Canter, the man you suspect had something to do with your father's disappearance. Abby saw Canter's name on a business paper in Cutter's office. Then we learned that Cutter's ship was in the harbor, but that he was sailing soon. So we sneaked aboard his ship to investigate."

Duncan crossed his arms over his chest and shook his head. "Go on."

"While we were there, we found a sea chest with your father's initials on it."

The Scotsman sat up straight, his eyes narrowing. "Keep talking, lad," he urged.

"Inside the chest was a letter to Mr. George Cutter. Apparently, he and your father were friends. And your father had asked Mr. Cutter to watch out for his new wife, Kalele. But that's not all we found. There was also a 'Last Will and Testament,' which we now know is the Cutter parents' real will. Why that sea varmint Cap'n Jim has it, we don't know."

Duncan jumped up and put a hand on Luke's shoulder. "But this doesn't prove that Lani is me sister. No one at the Cutter plantation ever heard of Kalele." He looked discouraged.

"But that's not all, Duncan! Just yesterday Abby and I went with Lani to her mother's hiding place, and Lani found a similar letter stored in a barrel there. She'd never seen it before, but it was a love letter written to Kalele. That's when Lani explained that her mother had changed her name 30 years ago to Naomi. And this letter was signed 'Ian MacIndou.'"

Understanding dawned in Duncan's eyes. "I have a sister," he said in an awed voice. "I wonder if me da ever knew her." Then eagerly he asked, "Do ye think it's too earrrly to wake the lass?"

Luke smiled at his enthusiasm. "It's a nice surprise, huh? Come on, I'll show you her hut."

Soon they stood at the opened door in shock.

"Looks like a tornado tore through here last night," Luke exclaimed. "Something's happened to Lani!"

Within minutes, they'd wakened Uncle Samuel and the Kendalls, who quickly discovered Abby was not in her bed either. Mrs. Kendall turned pale when she heard Lani was missing as well.

But Luke pulled Duncan aside. "Reese told Lani yesterday that Cap'n Jim Canter was asking about her mother."

Duncan's face darkened with anger. "Canter is still here on Kauai?"

"He must still be after the gold your father had," Luke said.

"Why would he take Abby and Lani?" Duncan asked. "There's no way for Canter to connect Lani with me da."

Luke corrected him. "The headstone was in the front yard yesterday when Canter came by. It has both of Lani's mother's names on it—'Naomi Kamana, once called Kalele.' Canter saw the headstone and must've known she was your father's wife. I bet he thinks Naomi passed on the gold to Lani before she died!"

Luke paced in agitation. *What did that cutthroat do with Abby?*

Duncan raked a hand through his hair, his face stern. "He must've taken the lassies to his ship!"

Mr. Kendall spoke up. "By the saints, if he sails with my daughter, I'll tear him limb from limb!" His voice boomed over the morning sounds of other families rising, and several men from nearby huts came over to find out what was wrong.

Within minutes one of the workers had harnessed two horses to a wagon. "Get in. We go to the harbor to stop him!" he yelled. Five men grabbed their machetes, sharp blades for cutting cane, and piled into the wagon. Abby's pa looked at Uncle Samuel. "Are you coming with us?"

Luke stopped pacing. "Wait! I don't think he'd take them to the harbor. If he thinks Lani has the gold, he'll force her to take him to it. And there's only one place she could lead him, one place she'd take him to give us time to find them! The secret hiding place."

Mr. Kendall looked desperately from Duncan to Luke. "I'm heading to the harbor. I can't bear the thought that he might take Abby from the island. Samuel, you coming with me?"

Uncle Samuel looked torn, but finally said, "Thomas, you've got plenty of men. I'll go with Luke and Duncan to the hiding place, just in case."

The wagon driver cracked a whip and the horses leapt to do his bidding, jerking the wagon forward. Abby's pa jumped on at the last minute and disappeared in a dust cloud as the horses galloped down the lane toward the harbor road.

Mrs. Kendall looked stricken with worry, and Sarah's face had paled. She clung to her ma's skirt, and Kini put one arm around her. "We'll search the grounds around here," Abby's ma said to Duncan and Uncle Samuel. "Just in case." She and the children headed out immediately.

Duncan, Uncle Samuel, and Luke rushed to the stables. There they discovered three horses missing and the groom tied up. "Someone hit me on the head," he said. A red welt on his forehead verified his words.

"The question is," Duncan said, "were there two men and they put Abby and Lani on one horse, or was it Canter alone with each girl on her own horse?"

Quickly the three mounted up and headed out after the tracks they discovered. In minutes Luke was sure Lani and Abby were leading Cap'n Jim to the secret hiding place.

And he silently thanked God that he knew just how to get there. He spurred his horse forward and took the lead, praying that Abby and Lani would be all right.

They rode hard and fast for an hour. When they let the horses walk to cool down, Duncan pulled his horse next to Luke's.

"I learned a bit while I was gone," Duncan said quietly. "The Kauai chief who was to marry Kalele was so outraged by her rrrunning off with me da that he vowed rrrevenge. So, laddie, that must be why Kalele changed her name to Naomi, and why me da and Kalele had to spend some time in their hiding place. She had to disappear so she could raise me sister in safety."

Luke nodded. "That's what Abby and I figured."

Duncan sighed. "Canter is a swine. He must've had a part in me da's death to have his sea chest." A moment later, he added, "But the Cutters must've been good Christian folks to take Kalele in all these years." He shook his head in wonder. "I can hardly believe Lani is me half sister. 'Tis a mirrracle to have family after all these years alone!"

But then his joy seemed to sour. "If Canter has touched a hairrr on either of me darrrlings' heads, I'll wring his worthless neck."

Only if you beat me to him, Luke thought angrily. *Hang on, Abby! We're coming.*

Without another word, the two automatically spurred their horses on to gallops, and Uncle Samuel followed suit.

Chapter Fifteen

Abby held the reins loosely now, after three hours of riding. The sun had just risen, bringing color to the somber landscape. She was pretty sure Lani had added a few miles to the original path they'd taken the day before because they'd passed several sights she didn't remember. *Lani is stalling for time,* she thought, *and hoping someone comes to our rescue.*

But the only one who knew the way to the hiding place was Luke. "Dear Lord," she whispered, "let him realize that's where we've gone. . . ."

"Get moving!" Cap'n Jim ordered with a wave of the pistol when Abby's horse stopped to crop grass.

Abby pulled the horse's head up with the reins and clucked for him to move. But the horse only snorted and yanked back on the reins, so Abby dug in her heels to urge it forward. When its ears went back in irritation, Abby felt the first tremor of fear.

Suddenly the horse reared back on two legs. Lani screamed, then clung to Abby, while Abby grabbed the saddle horn and held on with both hands and legs. But the backward momentum was too much for her. She slipped in the saddle, and her hands loosened. Her feet flew out of the stirrups, and the moment the horse's front hooves hit the ground again, Abby's grip was jarred loose. She and Lani tumbled off as the horse sprung forward.

Dazed, Abby lay in a cloud of slowly settling dust. Then she noticed a pain shooting through her head. "Lani," she said, unable to move.

"I'm here, Abby." Lani's face materialized, her sky blue eyes full of concern as she hovered over Abby. "Are you all right?"

"I think so . . . ." She tried to sit up but felt too dizzy.

"Lie still," Lani ordered. Abby saw her gaze up at the two mounted men with fury in her eyes. "She shouldn't have been here! This wouldn't have happened if it weren't for you."

"Shut yer trap!" Canter screamed. "No woman talks to me like that."

Abby's stomach clenched at the hatred in his voice. *He's ugly,* she thought, *with his oily balding head and fat belly. But even more, he's dangerous. His hate poisons everyone in his path. How are we going to escape him?* Abby wondered hopelessly as she lay in the dirt.

When Lani's face turned red at Canter's nasty words, Abby realized that the beautiful Hawaiian was angry enough to fight back. So Abby grabbed

Lani's hand and held on. "Lani, I'm feeling better now. Can you help me up?"

Instantly Lani's face softened. She bent down and put a hand behind Abby's back, lifting her gently to a sitting position.

Abby's head pounded. "I'm going to sit on that log for a minute so I can get my bearings."

Lani helped her over to the fallen tree while Dutch went after their horse. As they sat there, a light breeze wafted over them, surprising them with a sudden shower of white petals. Abby reached out and caught a plumeria blossom that had been shaken loose from overhead. She breathed in the heavenly, sweet fragrance.

Oh, Lord, she prayed, *thank You for reminding me of my poem . . . of the fact that You are the One with all the creative power in the universe. Nothing is too hard for You. Please help us remember and believe that.*

Dutch returned, and Canter surprised her by dismounting. Though he grumbled about the delay, he too sat down for a brief rest.

Five minutes later they were back on the trail, and now Abby could see they were among the ohi'a trees and quite close to Naomi's hut. When they emerged into the little clearing with the grass house, Canter chuckled low in his throat.

"See, Dutch," he called out, "stick with me and you'll be rich."

Lani slid off first and waited for Abby to

dismount. Immediately Canter came up behind Lani and rudely thrust her toward the ramshackle hut. "Open it," he growled.

Lani pushed open the door to her mother's hiding place and led them in.

What will she tell them? Abby thought, the blood surging through her temples. *There is no gold!*

As Abby entered and stood beside Lani, she saw her swallow nervously. *Oh, God, give Lani an idea to stall them—until Pa can rescue us!*

"Where is it?" Dutch shouted. He'd been silent most of the way, but Abby could clearly see the eagerness in his apple-cheeked face. Dutch was young, impatient, and quiet. In many ways, he appeared to be the opposite of James Canter: thin, not fat, and full headed, not bald. But the two men did have one thing in common—greed. As Ma would say, gold can make for strange bedfellows.

Canter took quick stock of the room and hurried over to the barrel in the corner. He tore off the board that lay on top and roared when he found it empty. Throwing the board on the dirt floor, he turned and yelled at Lani. "Where is it?"

This seemed to incite Dutch to a frenzy. "Where is it?" he echoed, apparently afraid they'd been cheated.

Lani pointed to the bedstead she and Abby had sat on just yesterday. "Try digging under the bed," she said simply. "The earth is hard packed because it's been there a long time."

That seemed to convince both Canter and Dutch, who couldn't wait to get their hands on easy wealth. "Start digging," Canter spat out.

"I ain't got no shovel," Dutch complained.

"You got a brain?" Canter sneered.

Dutch's cheeks flamed redder. "What do ya mean?"

"Well, use it. How about that fancy bowie knife ya always carry?"

Dutch snorted in disgust and picked up one end of the bed and flung it over. It went crashing on its side into the crates along the wall. He unsheathed a 10-inch, steel knife. Kneeling down on the dirt, he began stabbing the hard-packed earth over and over.

"Keep at it," Canter ordered as he, too, unsheathed a knife and cut some rope from the bed. He tied Abby's and Lani's hands behind their backs and made them sit in the empty half of the hut. Then he laid his gun on his knees and pulled a tin flask from his shirt pocket. Unscrewing the cap, he took a swig. "Want some?" he questioned Dutch.

Dutch smiled for the first time all morning as he took a swig. He'd been working nonstop for 20 minutes and had loosened a three-foot-wide space of rock-hard dirt. Now he dropped the knife in the churned-up earth and joined Canter for a break from the sweaty work. Between swills, the two men began daydreaming out loud about how they'd spend their riches.

Silently Lani gazed at Abby. Her aquamarine eyes flooded with tears. "I'm sorry my father's money got you into this," she whispered. What Abby saw next in Lani's eyes made her heart squeeze tight. Lani believed that when they found no gold, Canter would keep his word and make them pay.

Luke breathed a sigh of relief when he saw three horses tied to bushes in front of Naomi's hut. *Thank You, Jesus.* Duncan and Uncle Samuel reined in their horses 100 yards back and made their way stealthily toward the grass shack.

The door was open, so they circled around and waited, listening. Duncan motioned to Samuel with two fingers raised and mouthed the words, "Two men talking." Then he signed that he and Samuel should be the first two in, and Luke should follow.

Seconds later Duncan plunged through the open doorway and found Canter just starting to stand. Though the villain was taller than Duncan, he was taken by surprise. The angry Scotsman laid into him with fists flying. When his knuckles met with Canter's jaw, Duncan yelled, "Ye yellow-bellied varrrmint, ye killed me da!" *Whack!*

Abby's eyes bulged at the action.

Canter went crashing backward and sprawled on the dirt. "I don't know what yer talkin' about!"

Meanwhile, Uncle Samuel and Dutch were going at it, their height and weight pretty evenly matched. Sharing blows equally, they swung back and forth across Abby's vision.

When Duncan again accused Canter of murdering his father, Canter swore he didn't know what Duncan was talking about. Finally Abby couldn't stand his lies. "You do *too* know what he's talking about!" she yelled. "We found his father's sea chest in your cabin on board the *Beauty*. And the letter you stole, too!"

Canter looked at her through glazed eyes. Duncan's initial blow had taken some of the fight out of him. As the fat captain rolled from his stomach to his back, groaning in pain, anger burned in his eyes. "All right, I'll tell ya." He got up on his knees and swayed a moment. Then he stood up, his face twisted and dark. "The gold shoulda been mine 30 years ago. So what if I did what I had to? I hated that highfalutin' Scot!"

And with those words, Cap'n Jim lunged at Duncan. But Duncan was faster. His fist smashed into Canter's arrogant face and sent him flying backward through the air.

At the same moment, Uncle Samuel, with the help of Luke, finally subdued Dutch. They were busy tying him like a trussed-up turkey when

Canter crashed back to earth, smashing into the barrel.

With a giant *crack,* the barrel split open. All eyes turned toward it—and the sound of coins spilling out. For there, amid Canter's unconscious body, were dozens of gold coins! Shiny, yellow coins, spilling out in a river of tinkling sound.

Duncan, nursing sore knuckles, grinned. "Me da must've built a false bottom in the barrel!" Duncan stroked his chin and began to chuckle. "That's a cooper for ye. Me da was one smart man."

"Luke," he called, "will ye tie up this no-good rat fer me?"

Luke cut another piece of rope from the bed and began tying up Canter's hands, while Uncle Samuel hurried over to Abby and Lani and started untying Lani's ropes.

But Abby's eyes were riveted on Duncan, who had noticed something buried amid the river of gold coins. She watched him bend down on one knee and reach for something wrapped in a blue cloth. The Scotsman was quiet as he opened the cloth that now lay in his palm.

"What is it, Duncan?" Abby asked, still tied up but too engrossed in the unfolding drama to care much.

Duncan shook his head silently. He turned and held out his opened hand. There, in the center of his palm, lay an exquisitely carved elephant. Duncan's eyes flooded with tears. How many tears had the little boy in him cried for that elephant, she wondered. . . . How many years had he questioned if his father would keep his promise? If his father truly loved him or not? Duncan tenderly wrapped the carving in the cloth and tucked it into his vest pocket. She thought she heard him say, "Ye didna forget, Da."

Abby knew the elephant was all he'd ever hoped for from his father. She could hardly wait to tell Kini and Sarah how the story had finally ended.

Just then a deep voice growled from a few feet behind her, "Hand over the gold!"

Shocked, Abby turned to see Reese Cutter in the doorway. He held a gun, and it was drawn on Duncan.

Chapter Sixteen

Reese Cutter's dark eyes were riveted on the spilled gold coins.

Abby's mind spun in confusion. *What's Reese doing? He's holding the pistol on the wrong person—unless . . .*

Cap'n Jim, now conscious, looked up at Reese and began belly laughing. "What'd ya expect?" he asked the others. "This distinguished plantation owner is my partner!"

"Shut up!" Reese commanded.

But Cap'n Jim couldn't seem to shut up. The look on his face told Abby that he enjoyed the pain he was causing. "We've had a partnership ever since I helped him forge a new will to replace his parents' real will!" He laughed as if it were a joke. "And," he said contentedly, "I've owned him ever since."

Reese's gaze veered to Lani. He shook his head emphatically. "That's not true."

But Canter cackled. "I ought to know. I signed

the will as witness. That was my part of the deal . . . his was to use me as shipper ever since."

Abby gasped. "That's true! Luke and I saw the will. Cap'n Jim's name is on it. But Luke and I also found the original will in Ian's sea chest. It says the Cutter parents intended for the plantation to be left to the workers after three years." Abby turned anguished eyes on Reese. "Why did you steal it?"

The handsome, clean-cut Reese seemed to transform before her eyes. It was as if a veil was taken away, and his true self showed through. Even his voice was pitched deeper.

"My parents were fools—completely taken in by the natives. But I'm their son! *I* should get everything. It was *my* birthright, not the natives'." Reese turned to Canter. "You said you'd get rid of the old will for me." His eyes narrowed. "Why'd you keep it?"

Canter shrugged. "Never know when somethin' like that'll come in handy."

Anger blazed on Reese's face. "You dirty turncoat! You planned on blackmailing me with that, didn't you?"

Though his hands were tied, Canter's feet weren't. He kicked a coin and sent it rolling. "Ya gonna bellyache like a woman and let this money just sit here, or ya gonna untie me and help me get rid of these brats? The kids have snooped too much. We've got no choice now but to get rid of the lot of them. There's a ravine I passed aways back that should do nicely as their final resting place."

Abby's mind went blank with fear. *Is this how it will end for all of us, at the hands of these ruthless men?*

As Reese stepped out of the doorway and toward Cap'n Jim, Abby instinctively thrust out her leg. Intent on the gold, he tripped and sprawled forward. His pistol flew through the air and landed in the dirt just a foot from Luke. He dove for it!

Meanwhile Lani, now untied, lost no time. Reese lay sprawled face-first in the dirt, the wind knocked out of him. Lani jumped on his back and grabbed a fistful of his well-cut hair. A rapid rush of Hawaiian words spilled from her, and in between them, Abby heard her say, "Shame on you! Shame on you, Reese Cutter! Your parents must be turning over in their graves!"

Uncle Samuel followed her lead and also jumped on Reese's back, to help hold him down.

Duncan, meanwhile, gladly took the pistol from Luke and motioned for Luke to cut another length of rope and tie up Reese. Lani climbed off and hurried to untie Abby.

"Good move, little *keiki*," Lani gushed proudly as she loosened Abby's knots. "We didn't do too badly fighting the men, eh?"

"Oh, crimony, ya make me sick," Cap'n Jim complained as he listened to the girls. But Duncan grabbed him by the scruff of his neck and dragged him out the door.

Canter spewed curses at Reese as he passed. "You stupid fool!" he screamed, trying to kick Reese as he went by. "You let a *girl* do you in!"

Abby basked in the words.

Duncan herded Canter and Dutch out and tied them to their horses like sacks of potatoes hanging down on each side of the saddle. Uncle Samuel did the same to Reese, who complained loudly of the undignified treatment. Until the others were mounted, there was no risk that they would get away.

Inside the hut, Luke bent down and picked up the bowie knife Dutch had left in the churned-up earth. "Kini will love this to flay fish," he said to Abby.

She remembered how Kini had longed for a pocketknife like Luke's from the first time they had met on Lanai. "That's thoughtful of you, Luke."

"Luke," Lani said, "would you help me turn the bed back over? It's sad seeing Mother's hiding place like this."

"Sure, Lani." Luke jumped up and did it for her. "I'll see if Duncan needs any help."

As he exited, Lani sat down. "It's been quite a

day, and it's not even noon," she said to Abby. "Worst of all, I'm still in my nightdress. This is very humiliating."

Uncle Samuel, who was just entering the shack, must have heard her. He took off his long-sleeved shirt. Standing in his undershirt and pants, he gently draped his shirt around Lani's shoulders, then left without a word.

Abby couldn't believe her eyes. Her absent-minded uncle had noticed Lani's need, and now Lani was wiping away tears. "He's so sweet," she said, "and kind."

Abby sat down next to her. "Yes, and he's smart, too. He always says there's a reason for everything God does. I guess there was a purpose even in that rotten Cap'n Jim looking for your father's gold. It brought you and Duncan together in the end. . . . I suppose Cap'n Jim was right about one thing. Your father did leave Kalele his gold."

Duncan walked in and heard her final comment. "Ye're right, lassie. He did leave us gold, but this is what I treasure most." He withdrew the blue cloth from his pocket, kneeled in front of Lani, and handed her the cloth-wrapped package.

She smiled at him and opened the cloth. Picking up the delicate elephant carving, she uttered a contented sigh. "I knew our father was a sailor who also carved wood. I have a little bird that he whittled for Mother. But I never knew his English name. Mother called him 'Kamana,' which means carpenter. I always thought she did that because he worked with wood." She gazed tenderly at Duncan, then handed the elephant back to him.

"And I knew he was a cooper, a barrel maker," Duncan said. "But I didn't know anything about Kalele . . . and I never guessed in me wildest drrreams that I had a sister—especially not one as lovely as ye, Lani. I suppose if the truth be told," Duncan admitted, "the greatest gift me da left me wasn't this elephant. It was ye, me own sister, to love."

With a cry of delight, Lani threw herself into Duncan's arms. When she pulled back, her eyes were shining. "I'm so happy to have a brother, too."

"Well, lassie, there's much to discuss."

Luke walked in, whistling. He swung an empty saddlebag by his side, then crouched down and began filling it with gold. "It's about time to wrap up this mystery, wouldn't you say, Duncan? There are a few more important things to do now."

"Aye, lad. Like delivering the varrrmints to the local judge."

Luke gave Abby a wink. "Nay," he said, mimicking a Scottish brogue, "I'd say brrreakfast is the next prrressing task."

He began raking in the coins double-time, and Abby bent down to help. "I know," she said, "you can't help it. You're just a prisoner of your stomach."

Luke sat back on his heels, assessing her. "And *you* can't help seeing the best in people, Abby Kendall. At first Reese Cutter seemed nice, but his biggest motivation wasn't to help people. It was only to get what he wanted. Remember, the Bible says a man reaps what he sows. And the ways of the unrighteous always lead to—"

But he never got to finish because Abby tackled him, tickling his growling stomach without mercy.

Chapter Seventeen

They rode hard and fast to the plantation, knowing Pa and Ma would be frantic with worry. In two and a half hours, they made it back. As they trotted up to the big house, everyone saw them and rushed to greet them.

A dusty and exhausted-looking Pa lifted Abby from the saddle and hung on tightly. Then he handed her over to Ma's waiting arms.

"Abby," Sarah said, her blue eyes round and swimming with tears, "ever since we knew you were kidnapped, I've had a really bad stomachache."

Abby gave her irritating little sister a giant hug. "I love you, Sarah. I'm sorry you worried, but God kept me safe."

"We prayed," Sarah exclaimed. "Me and Kini prayed together."

Abby reached over and gave their Hawaiian friend a bear hug, too.

Hoku and Malama, who'd also joined the search parties in Abby and Lani's absence, stood with mouths open when they saw Reese strung up like a Christmas turkey. Duncan quickly explained the situation with the wills, while Abby ran to her hut to retrieve the original one the Cutter parents had written.

When she returned, Malama and Hoku read it together. Then, teary-eyed, they gave an order for the rest of the workers to be gathered. Within the hour, the crowd of loyal Hawaiian workers were all sitting on the Cutters' lawn to hear the pronouncement of the will. Lani read the words aloud:

"For the first three years after our deaths, Reese will run the plantation and collect the profits. This will fund the travels he so longs for. During this time, he will train Hoku and Malama to be overseers to run the business, although they know most everything already. At the end of three years, Reese shall hand over the deed to the land and plantation to the Hawaiian workers. We wish for Reese to always have a place here in the mansion. He should be considered family to the Hawaiians, just as they are family to us. This is why we want them to own the land again and run their own business."

Tears welled up in Malama's eyes. "I was right. Mr. and Mrs. Cutter, they had Hawaiian hearts, full of *aloha*. Now we go from being poor to being rich, from being almost slaves to being free. We be treated like family," she said, taking the will from Lani and holding it high, "and these good people meant to give us our homeland all along."

A wild cheer went up, and a feast was planned for the very next day—to celebrate the Hawaiians' new life.

But in the midst of the festive moment, Hoku and five other *kanakas* approached Duncan and Pa. Hoku shook his head sadly. Abby overheard him say, "I will deliver Mr. Reese and these other two men to the judge. But this is a sad day for us. Reese used to be a good son." His voice broke as he told Pa about the Cutter parents and all they had done for the Hawaiians. "The Bible warns us that bad company corrupts good character. In Reese's case," he finished sadly, "it was true."

As the men prepared to leave with their captives for the judge, Abby walked over to Reese Cutter. She removed the only key to the vault from around his neck and took it back to Malama. "I imagine some of the money he stores in there belongs to you and the others, since he's had the plantation three years longer than his parents intended."

Malama nodded. "His parents left him a fortune. How I wish Mr. Reese had gone traveling as he always wanted and not gotten mixed up with that bad man."

Abby's heart was heavy. Evidently there had been much good in Reese—until he'd turned down the wrong path. Instantly she remembered words her mother had read from the Bible: "[Love] does not rejoice in unrighteousness, but rejoices with the truth" (1 Corinthians 13:6).

Lord, Abby prayed, *though I'm glad the truth came out, I'm sad for Reese. Sad that he chose the wrong path.*

The happy throng of Hawaiians moved around her, but in spite of the crowd, Abby suddenly sensed God's presence.

LOVE NEVER FAILS. The words of 1 Corinthians 13:8 penetrated Abby's mind like the light of a torch in a black cave.

Oh, Lord, You're right! Though Reese failed, Your love won't fail Reese. I will pray for him to turn back to You. Maybe someday he can be the man You planned for him to be.

I AM NOT WILLING THAT ANY SHOULD PERISH. NOW IS THE DAY OF SALVATION.

"Now, Lord?" she whispered, sensing what God wanted. "But I'm just a kid. . . ." Yet the urgent feeling inside would not relent. Abby sighed and started toward Reese.

He was still slung over the saddle like a sack of potatoes. His jet-black hair covered his eyes. But when Abby's feet and sandals appeared below him, his head shot up. It was red. *From all the blood rushing to it, or from anger?* she wondered.

"What do you want?" he said low in his throat. "Come to gloat?"

Abby swallowed and shook her head. "I came to tell you that . . . God loves you. His love won't fail you. And . . . I'm praying for you."

Reese's jaw grew slack as Abby's soft answer struck him. A swirl of emotion swept through his eyes. She saw a mixture of surprise, shame, then the barest flicker of gratitude. Was that a sheen of moisture in his eyes?

A long sigh escaped him and he nodded slightly before resuming his miserable upside-down position. Abby gingerly patted his shoulder, then went to find Duncan. It was time to let Reese Cutter sit up.

Chapter Eighteen

The next day everyone busily prepared for the feast. Abby joined the women in the big house and made three mango cobblers. Kini and Sarah spent hours threading plumeria-blossom leis, while Luke and the men dug an *imu,* a pit, early in the morning to roast the pig.

Hoku and the others returned as night began to fall. Malama gave orders for oiled *tiki* torches to be set up all over the wide lawn. Soon tables were placed there, and many women carried out steaming trays of tempting food.

A 100-pound pig had been wrapped in banana leaves and red-hot stones and buried deep in the earth to bake for many hours. Now the ground was opened. The delicious scent drew everyone close. Abby knew that the meat would be so tender it would fall off the bone. She glanced over at Luke. His eyes were riveted on a platter of roasted pig being carried to the table, and she could almost see him drool.

Ukuleles were brought out by many of the Hawaiians, and tunes began against the background of happy voices. Abby sat on spread-out blankets with her family, Kini, Luke, Lani, Duncan, Malama, and Hoku. When Uncle Samuel borrowed an ukulele from a friendly young man, he created an impromptu song about a heroine named Lani.

> "*She captures villains by sitting on their backs,*
> *And keeps them in line by giving them whacks.*
> *Her heart is so brave, she's never felt fear,*
> *But her enemies do, and she leaves 'em in tears!*"

Duncan laughed and poked Lani in the ribs. "That's me sister, all rrright."

Abby watched Lani lean over and say something to Duncan. Soon they were deep in discussion, but every now and again, Lani would glance up and smile at Uncle Samuel. Abby was amazed that each time she did, Uncle Samuel's ears blushed pink.

"Come!" Malama cried out. "We be thanking our dear Lord for this wonderful day—the day the land came back to us." Then everyone bowed, and Hoku led them in a prayer of thanksgiving. People soon milled about the tables, piling up the hot, mouthwatering food for their late-night dinner.

Abby sat near Ma, Pa, and Uncle Samuel so she could hear their conversation. Now, with all the

changes at the plantation, she wondered what Pa
had in mind for their family.

"Hoku told me that it takes two years before the
first sugar crop is harvested," Uncle Samuel said.
"So a sugar plantation requires enough money to
support everyone without an income for at least
that long."

Pa nodded. "And with the gold rush in California, soon there won't be enough workers to run
plantations. In fact, the labor shortage has already
hit," he said with a grimace. "Going into sugar
doesn't look like an open door to me."

Duncan finished a bite of food. "Are ye saying
that ye won't be staying?"

"Don't see that it can work," Pa answered, a little
down in the mouth.

"Grrreat!" Duncan responded happily. "I need ye
on the ship with me. I already have me first order to
ship sugar to China. I picked up the job while investigating a few days ago. And I want ye and Samuel
for a crew. We'll split the shipping profits three
ways and be equal partners. But I have to leave
soon." His face glowed with hope.

Pa looked at Ma questioningly. She smiled and
nodded. "I thought I wanted a permanent home,"
she said, "but after Abby's kidnapping, I realized
that what I want most is a permanent family. As
long as we're together, that's enough home for me."

Pa gave Ma a huge hug. Then he and Uncle
Samuel got up and shook hands with Duncan, who

put his big paw over theirs. "Well, 'twill be nice to be a family together. Lani's already agreed to join us."

When Ma instantly clapped her hands in delight, Abby realized how lonely it must have been for Ma, without a woman friend.

Uncle Samuel's gaze quickly veered to Lani, who met it with a smile. Abby watched her uncle's ears turn pink again.

"Well," Abby said in amazement to Luke, "I can hardly believe it. We get to see more of the world!" She and Luke joined Sarah in dancing to the happy Hawaiian music that flowed all around them.

But Abby couldn't help noticing that Kini sat to the side, quietly stroking the sleeping puppy. He was staring off into the distance, as if remembering another time. *I wonder if he's thinking about home,* she thought. *If only he could go home, then each of us could have our dream.*

Later, when the moon sailed high overhead and caught in the boughs of the mango trees, Malama came to say good night.

"We will be leaving in the morning," Ma explained.

Abby was sure she saw a flicker of pain cross Malama's face. Malama turned to Hoku, her expression sad. "We will miss you Kendalls, Luke, Duncan, and Kini. Charlotte, I be taking over where you leave off with the *keikis*. I will hire a teacher to come teach here. First thing we do is open up the school again with some of the money we found in the vault."

Ma gave her a hug, and Hoku shook the men's hands. Then Malama rubbed noses with Abby, Sarah, and Luke. But when she got to Kini, she kneeled at his feet and looked in his dark brown eyes. "Kini, you are dear to me. I never have my own *keikis*." The kind Hawaiian woman tapped her chest. "My heart be very sore when you leave."

Kini grabbed Malama's work-roughened hand. "I be Kini, son of Kono, son of Mako. But my family, they follow the old gods. I cannot go back there. I want to follow the God of Abby and you. I decide I stay here with you. The islands be my home."

Malama's eyes grew wide, and Hoku quickly dropped to one knee to stare in Kini's face. "Son of Kono, son of Mako?" Hoku grabbed Kini by the shoulder. "My brother, the one who made this necklace for me, his name is Kono. My father is Mako! Does your family, your father, live on Lanai?" he asked, his face incredulous.

"Yes, it be so," Kini answered, nodding.

Malama grabbed Kini to her chest and held him tightly. "Kini, that why you be part of our heart. You be one of our family! You be our nephew. But we never meet you because your father and grandfather move far away many years ago."

Hoku drew Kini into an embrace and began to cry. "The Lord brought you here, Kini. We be your family, and one day we go to Lanai together and tell your father and mother the Good News of Jesus. Together we will say, 'Don't worship gods of wood and stone anymore.'"

Abby felt tears on her cheeks and wiped them away quickly. All their dreams had come true. Kini had found a home!

But Sarah burst into tears at the news, waking Sandy. Ma put an arm around Sarah, comforting and patting her. "We'll come back to visit, darling. Don't cry. This is wonderful for Kini."

Sarah sniffed hard and nodded as she bent down to pick up a squirming Sandy. "I know." Then, with the puppy squished between them, Sarah and Kini hugged a long time. As they pulled apart, Sandy barked and Sarah added, "I told everyone Hoku's necklace was just like yours!"

Duncan, who'd been listening intently, patted Kini's shoulder. "It seems, lad, that both of us got our hearts' desire." Kini left Sarah's side and threw his thin arms around Duncan's waist. The one-eyed Scotsman gazed over Kini to Abby. When he winked, she grinned. At least there would be no good-byes for her and Duncan tomorrow. And soon she'd be sailing off on another adventure—to the mysterious land of China!

Abby drank in the happy faces of Luke and Sarah, Ma and Pa, Uncle Samuel, and now the lovely Lani, too. *Together with God,* she thought, *each one of these is my heart's desire.*

KAUAI

OAHU
Kailua

MOLOKAI

Lahaina

MAUI

HAWAII

N

THE
HAWAIIAN
ISLANDS

*Don't miss the next exciting adventure in
the South Seas Adventures series:*

Abby
King's
Ransom

When Abby and her crew sail to Shanghai,
what do they pluck from the South China Sea
that changes Abby's life? And will they encounter the deadly pirate king, Zai Ching, who
terrorizes these waters? You don't want to miss
King's Ransom!

Hawaiian People, Places, and Words

Follow these two simple rules to say Hawaiian words correctly:

1. Don't end a syllable with a consonant. For example, Honolulu should be pronounced Ho-no-lu-lu, not Hon-o-lu-lu.

2. Say each vowel in a word. The vowels generally are pronounced like this:
   a as in daughter
   e as in prey
   i as in ring
   o as in cold
   oo as in tool

aloha—word of welcome or farewell, a type of unconditional love shared

Great Mahele—land division meant to distribute the king's land among commoners and royalty

haole—white foreigner, usually a Caucasian

Honolulu—Hawiian city and port on the island of Oahu

Kailua—Hawaiian city on the island of Oahu

kanaka—Hawaiian man or worker

kapu—something that is taboo or off limits

Kauai—the northernmost of the large islands in the Hawaiian chain

keiki—child

kiawe—tree with sharp thorns which was brought to Hawaii in the 1820s

ko—sugarcane

koa—the largest native tree found in Hawaii's forests

konane—Hawaiian rock game similar to checkers

Lanai—small island near Maui and Molokai

lanai—porch

lehua—flower that grows on the ohiʻa-*lehua* tree

luau—Hawaiian feast

mahalo—thank you

menehune—the legendary "little people" of Kauai who create mischief

muumuu—a Hawaiian dress

nani-hair—pretty hair

Oahu—a large island in the Hawaiian chain

ohiʻa—a tree with bright red flowers

pikake—small, very fragrant white flower used to make leis *poi*—a Hawaiian staple made from the taro plant

puka shells—small shells with little holes in the middle, often used to make necklaces

tapa—cloth made from the bark of the paper mulberry tree

tiki torch—a torch set on a long pole driven into the earth, often used as lighting at celebrations

wahine—woman or female (also women)

Nautical Words

bow—front of ship

bulkhead—raised portion on deck

gangplank—a movable bridge for boarding or leaving a ship at a pier

hatch—a door in the deck of a ship

helm—a lever or wheel used to control the rudder of a ship for steering

hull—the frame of a ship

jetty—a protecting frame of a pier

mast—wooden beam that holds up the sails

masthead—the top of a mast

porthole—an opening with a cover in the side of a ship

reefing—to reduce the area of a sail by rolling or folding

rigging—lines and chains used aboard a ship

schooner—a sailing vessel with at least two masts

shrouds—a set of ropes that stretch from a ship's side to a masthead

skiff—a small boat

stern—the back of a ship

About the Author

Pamela Walls, a freelance writer, backpacked with girlfriends on the tropical "Garden Island" of Kauai. This Pacific paradise, Pamela says, is famous for its waterfalls, canyons, and brilliant flowers.

"We roamed the island in search of adventure and weren't disappointed when we found a waterfall made famous for its rock slide. We climbed the face of the falls and sailed down the water slide, flying 15 feet through the air to land with a splash in the dark green pool below. But while we were climbing out, we watched young people at the top pour a whole bottle of dish soap down the falls. The pool below instantly bubbled up with suds, and people began landing in a gigantic white bubble bath. For a few minutes it looked like fun, but soon the pretty pond became scummy and polluted.

"That pool could have used some of the extra water from the next place we visited—Mount Wai'ale'ale. The name means 'Overflowing Water' for a good reason: it gets over 50 feet of rainfall a year! Tourists come to see 'the wettest spot on earth,' but we had arrived for a night of camping with only a tiny pup tent. Luckily, a troop of Boy Scouts was setting up camp at the same time—and they had come prepared. Kindly inviting us to share their baked beans, I was shocked to recognize someone I knew behind their leader's rain-fogged spectacles . . . my high school biology teacher! Since graduation, I'd never run into him back home in California, but now I had bumped into him on a mountaintop 2,400 miles away!

"While I might have been surprised by this 'chance encounter,' God surely wasn't. Proverbs 16:9 says, 'In his heart a man plans his course, but the Lord determines his steps.' For many years I was just like this proverb, trying to plan my own course. Although I had plenty of exciting adventures, I knew something was still missing from my life. Searching for happiness, I tried things that looked fun. But it was like I was pouring soap down the waterfall inside me. Somehow my heart had become scummy. Thank goodness God allowed this so I could see I needed to be cleaned on the inside!

"One night I cried out to Him, asking Him to cleanse me, forgive me, and help me live for Him. That's when everything changed. His river of living water poured in, washing away the scummy past and making all things new. He set me on a heavenly course. And as if this weren't enough, God also gave me my heart's desires: a family, a job I love, good friends. Sometimes it feels like I live in the 'wettest spot on earth' because His love continues to pour into me every day!

"So I've learned that no matter where you live—whether on a garden island or in a busy city—paradise isn't a location. It's a place in the heart."

Jesus stood and said in a loud voice, "If anyone is thirsty, let him come to me and drink. Whoever believes in me, as the Scripture has said, streams of living water will flow from within him." By this he meant the Spirit, whom those who believed in him were later to receive.

John 7:37-39